Augmented Reality

TOM SWIFT
INVENTORS' ACADEMY

-BOOK 6-
Augmented Reality

VICTOR APPLETON

Aladdin
NEW YORK LONDON TORONTO SYDNEY NEW DELHI

This book is a work of fiction. Any references to historical events, real people, or real places are used fictitiously. Other names, characters, places, and events are products of the author's imagination, and any resemblance to actual events or places or persons, living or dead, is entirely coincidental.

ALADDIN

An imprint of Simon & Schuster Children's Publishing Division

1230 Avenue of the Americas, New York, New York 10020

First Aladdin paperback edition March 2021

Text copyright © 2021 by Simon & Schuster, Inc.

Cover illustration copyright © 2021 by Kevin Keele

TOM SWIFT, TOM SWIFT INVENTORS' ACADEMY, and related logos are trademarks of Simon & Schuster, Inc.

Also available in an Aladdin hardcover edition.

All rights reserved, including the right of reproduction in whole or in part in any form.

ALADDIN and related logo are registered trademarks of Simon & Schuster, Inc.

For information about special discounts for bulk purchases, please contact Simon & Schuster Special Sales at 1-866-506-1949 or business@simonandschuster.com.

The Simon & Schuster Speakers Bureau can bring authors to your live event.

For more information or to book an event contact the Simon & Schuster Speakers Bureau at 1-866-248-3049 or visit our website at www.simonspeakers.com.

Cover designed by Heather Palisi

Interior designed by Mike Rosamilia

The text of this book was set in Adobe Caslon Pro.

Manufactured in the United States of America 0221 OFF

10 9 8 7 6 5 4 3 2 1

Library of Congress Cataloging-in-Publication Data

Names: Appleton, Victor, author.

Title: Augmented reality / Victor Appleton.

Description: First Aladdin hardcover edition. | New York : Aladdin, [2021] | Series: Tom Swift Inventors' Academy ; 6 | Audience: Ages 8 to 12. | Summary: Tom Swift Inventors' Academy is hosting an Invention Olympics, but Tom suspects that the crew filming a new reality show about the academy may be planning something nefarious.

Identifiers: LCCN 2020030069 (print) | LCCN 2020030070 (eBook) | ISBN 9781534468894 (paperback) | ISBN 9781534468900 (hardcover) | ISBN 9781534468917 (eBook)

Subjects: CYAC: Inventors—Fiction. | Contests—Fiction. | Reality television programs—Fiction. | Television—Production and direction—Fiction. | Schools—Fiction. | Friendship—Fiction. | Science fiction.

Classification: LCC PZ7.A652 Aug 2021 (print) | LCC PZ7.A652 (eBook) | DDC [Fic]—dc23

LC record available at https://lccn.loc.gov/2020030069

LC eBook record available at https://lccn.loc.gov/2020030070

Contents

1

The Augmented Expedition

I STEPPED INTO THE GYM AND SCANNED THE area. A few students sat on the bleachers. Some watched two members of the fencing team facing off, foils at the ready. Others chatted quietly or finished their homework last-minute before school began. Luckily, none of them seemed to be interested in my destination.

I casually strolled across the floor, heading toward the end of the single set of bleachers. I adjusted my glasses and looked at the seated students. I didn't bother glancing at the fencers; their masks would definitely block my facial recognition program.

That's right, I was testing my brand-new augmented reality glasses. You see, I had almost all of the academy students in my address book, so it was easy to add their faces to my program.

As I moved closer to the bleachers, small green squares appeared around the students' faces. Their names floated under those open boxes. Simone Mosby chatted with Alicia Wilkes. Evan Wittman sat alone, reading something on his tablet.

Okay, their names didn't *really* float next to these unsuspecting students. That was the *augmented* part of my augmented reality glasses. You see, my program projected the images onto my glasses so that only I could see them. The boxes continued to float next to the students even though I kept moving. It was very cool. In fact, I felt kind of like James Bond or Jason Bourne. Except their spy glasses might list a bunch of deadly facts about the subject. I imagined an additional list of stats floating beside Evan's face: *international assassin, wanted by Interpol, deadly with nunchucks.*

As I moved closer to the bleachers, Evan glanced up from his tablet. "Cool glasses, Tom," he said casually, instead of attacking me with nunchucks. "What do they do?"

"I'll tell you later," I replied as I continued toward my destination. "I'm still beta testing them."

Evan gave a knowing nod and went back to his tablet.

At any other school, I would've looked weird walking around wearing oversize safety glasses with wires leading down to a controller and power pack clipped to my belt. Okay, I'm sure I looked weird here, too. But at the Swift Academy of Science and Technology, it wasn't unusual for students to test their inventions on school grounds. You might see drones flying down the halls one day and green smoke billowing out of the chemistry lab the next. You never knew what strange and exciting things you'd come across at this school.

Today, I wasn't just testing my latest invention—I was also helping my best friend, Noah Newton, with his. That's why I made my way to the back of the bleachers. I was using my glasses to assist Noah with his own augmented reality invention. And I wasn't the only one. Noah had created a cool app that most of the academy students were helping him test.

I ducked behind the bleachers and adjusted my glasses. Scanning the dark and dusty area, I quickly spotted exactly what I was looking for: a cartoon pork chop slowly spun as it hovered just above the floor under the bleachers. It wasn't a real pork chop, obviously, but one I could see only using my glasses.

I dug out my phone and accessed Noah's *Feed the Beast* app. The program activated the camera, and I held up my phone so I could see the pork chop hovering on the screen. Using the app, I'd be able to see the cartoon hunk of meat even if I wasn't wearing my glasses.

My thumb moved toward the app's Collect button, but the pork chop disappeared before I could capture it. I spun around to see that I wasn't alone. A thin boy with curly brown hair held his own phone in front of him. I recognized the student, even as my glasses drew a square around his face and flashed a label: Terry Stephenson.

"Not so swift, Tom Swift," Terry said with a grin. "I found this one yesterday." Terry ducked his head as he stepped out from under the bleachers and disappeared from sight.

I closed Noah's app and shot him a text. **Someone found the one under the bleachers.**

Cool, Noah replied. **Keep looking.**

Hurrying away from the bleachers, I made my way to the gym doors, scanning the ceiling just in case Noah had hidden any other loot up there.

Noah had created a cool phone app that hid all kinds of cartoon food items all over the school. There were barrels of apples, cartoon fish, and even oversize cherries, just like in that old-school video game, *Pac-Man*. You couldn't see the items unless you were looking through your phone's camera, using his app.

Noah had made the app available to all the academy students so everyone could play. The object of the game was to go around the school and collect as many of the items as you could. The student who collected the most loot won for the day.

That wasn't the coolest part of the game, though. Every day after school, if you went outside and aimed your phone at the sky, you would be able to see a giant beast tromping toward the Swift Academy building. When it got close enough, all of the students who'd gathered loot could launch it toward the creature. If enough people collected enough food and successfully launched their cache into the monster's mouth, the beast

5

would be satisfied and it wouldn't destroy the school. That's right. Noah had created a cool program where a monster demolished the Swift Academy building. It looked amazing and pretty realistic.

Since Noah's app had launched three days before, the beast had torn down the school every time. And as cool as that was to watch, it also meant that not enough students had collected enough loot. Today looked like there was a pretty good chance that would change, though. Every day the app was live, more and more students could be seen roaming the halls with their phones out in front of them—even more than thirteen- and fourteen-year-olds usually do.

I stepped out of the gym and checked my watch. It was almost time for first period. I had just enough time to get to my locker, put away my glasses, and head to algebra. I'd help Noah grab more food items during lunch. Maybe today would be the day that we finally succeeded in feeding the beast!

I continued to test my glasses as I headed for my locker. They correctly identified Kevin Ryan, Mia Trevino, and Tony Garret. Unfortunately, they identified Jamal Watts as his sister, Shandra. I'd have to check my address book to make sure I had their photos right. Otherwise, my program wasn't able to tell the difference with a strong family resemblance.

I reached my locker and began dialing in my lock's combination.

"Attention, Swift Academy students," came Mr. Davenport's voice over the intercom system. "Noah Newton and Tom Swift, report to my office right away."

I sighed and reset my padlock. It looked like I was going to be late for algebra.

As I made my way to the principal's office, I got the usual jabs any student might have received after such a public announcement. They weren't too bad, especially considering my last name matches the name of the school.

There's a very good reason for that. My father, Tom Swift Sr., created the school with the profits from his nearby tech company, Swift Enterprises. However, ever since I started at the academy, I've done my best to be just another student. I don't want any special treatment from teachers or students. So far, that had worked out just fine.

When I entered the front office, Noah was already there sitting in one of the chairs by the school office manager's desk.

Ms. Lane smiled and nodded in the direction of my friend. "Just have a seat. Mr. Davenport will be with you in a moment."

I plopped down in the chair next to Noah's. "What do you think this is about?" I whispered.

Noah sighed and shook his head. "Isn't it obvious? Davenport's going to shut down my app." He rolled his eyes. "He probably thinks it's too *disruptive*."

I shrugged. "You never know. It might be something else."

Noah smirked and gave me a skeptical look. "One of the last times we were here was because of an app. What else could it be?"

My friend had a point. Once, Noah and I, along with our friends Samantha Watson and Amy Hsu, came to see Mr. Davenport because of an app Amy had created. It was a cool program that let students know when teachers were going to give a pop quiz. Now *that* app was disruptive . . . to the teachers' lesson plans, at least. Even though Noah's app did have kids' faces buried in their phones a little more than usual, I didn't think it was actually disruptive.

Something buzzed on Ms. Lane's desk and Mr.

Davenport's voice blared out of a small speaker. "Send them in, please," he said.

As Noah and I stood and headed back, Ms. Lane gave us a nod and a half-grin that seemed meant to wish us luck.

When we reached the principal's office, I was surprised to see that he wasn't alone. A blond woman in a bright red sweater sat in one of the four chairs in front of Mr. Davenport's desk. She turned and smiled at us as we filed in.

"Mr. Newton. Mr. Swift," Mr. Davenport said. He pointed to the chairs. "Please take a seat."

As we settled down, the principal stood. "Now, Mr. Newton, I was about to put the brakes on this . . . *Feed the Beast* app of yours."

My best friend gave me a *What did I tell you?* look before addressing the principal. "What if people just used it before school and during lunch?"

Mr. Davenport chuckled. "You're not listening, Mr. Newton. I said I was *about* to put the brakes on it."

Noah opened his mouth to debate some more, but then caught himself. "Oh," he said, relaxing a little. He'd clearly had an argument all ready to go.

The principal gestured to the woman. "But Ms. Jensen here talked me out of it."

The woman turned and extended a hand to us. "Purely for selfish reasons, I assure you," she said. "I'm Holly Jensen, the new head of PR at Swift Enterprises."

As I shook her hand, I was glad she said she was new. I didn't know everyone who worked at my father's company, for sure, but it would've been embarrassing if I had already met her and forgotten.

"How do you know about my app?" Noah asked. "It's just for the students and it's only been live for a few days now."

"Oh, I poke around here and there, talking to a few students and teachers," Ms. Jensen replied with a sly smile. "I wouldn't be good at my job if I didn't stay on top of all the exciting new innovations you little geniuses come up with." She stood, becoming quite animated. "And I think your app would be perfect to showcase at the upcoming . . . wait for it . . . Inventors' Olympics!"

Noah and I glanced at each other. "Wait, what?" I asked.

Ms. Jensen grinned and glanced around. "You two are the first students to find out the big news! In two

10

weeks, instead of Mr. Edge's invention convention, Mr. Davenport has graciously allowed Swift Enterprises to put on a display of all the academy students' inventions, which will be open to the public!"

Mr. Edge, our engineering teacher, holds a monthly showcase he calls the invention convention—a chance for students to show off their inventing skills. It's pretty informal; we meet in the cafeteria during lunch. But it's really cool to see all the creative inventions students have been building. I'd never thought of it being open to the public before. It was a good idea scheduling this new event to replace the upcoming invention convention. Most of the students were already well on their way to getting their inventions ready anyway.

"We thought it would be great advertising for the school," Ms. Jensen continued. She tapped her chin with one finger. "The only issue is . . . how do we show off your app to a large crowd of people? Could you get video footage somehow?"

My mind started racing. This was the kind of challenge I loved. Give me a problem with set parameters and I'm good to go!

I smiled and sat up straighter. "I think we can," I said, tapping my glasses, before explaining how they let me see the same virtual objects from Noah's app. "I bet we can rig some kind of filter that goes in front a camera lens."

"Oh yeah," Noah agreed with a grin. "For sure."

Ms. Jensen leaned closer to look at my glasses. "I thought those were a bit odd for a prescription pair."

Mr. Davenport shook his head. "I guess I'm just so used to seeing students wearing crazy contraptions, I didn't think to ask."

"You can try them if you like," I offered. "You can see how they identify everyone in the room. I'm thinking they would be great for a new student or teacher. It's like everyone would be wearing a virtual name tag." I began to remove the glasses. "Too bad there are no *Feed the Beast* items in here for you to see—"

I was interrupted by Noah nudging me. "Uh, about that . . ." He nodded toward a filing cabinet in the corner of the office.

I slid the glasses back on and turned toward the corner. A large cartoon pineapple hovered above the cabinet. My eyes widened. I couldn't believe I'd missed it before.

Mr. Davenport crossed his arms. "Mr. Newton . . . you

did not plant one of those virtual items in my office."

Noah shrugged. "You have to admit, it's a great hiding place."

I gave the glasses to Ms. Jensen, being careful to hold the trailing power pack beside her. She laughed when she spotted the cartoon fruit. "Amazing."

Noah pulled out his phone and pulled up his app. He held it up so Mr. Davenport could see the pineapple on the screen, then tapped a button in the app and the pineapple disappeared.

Ms. Jensen returned my glasses. "Okay, cards on the table," she said, leaning against Mr. Davenport's desk. "I had an ulterior motive for asking if your app could be recorded."

Noah and I glanced at each other. "Okay," Noah said.

"It involves another wonderful PR idea," she added.

Mr. Davenport sighed. "This one, I'm not so crazy about."

Ms. Jensen playfully shooed him with one hand. "Do either of you watch shows like *Camped Out* or *Squatch Hunters*?"

I shook my head, but Noah's eyes lit up. "I love *Camped Out*! It's hilarious."

Even though I hadn't watched them, I had certainly heard of both popular television shows. *Camped Out* was a reality show that had several teenagers from different backgrounds staying in a summer camp. They have these crazy competitions, and then vote someone out of camp every week. The last one in camp wins a big prize or something. *Squatch Hunters* was another reality show, but this one followed around a group of real-life Bigfoot hunters, "squatch" being short for Sasquatch.

"Well, I'm friends with the producer of both shows," Ms. Jensen continued. "I pitched him the idea of doing a reality show about Swift Academy, and he loved it."

"Sweet," Noah said, glancing at me with a big grin on his face.

I gave half a smile back.

Ms. Jensen placed her hands on our shoulders. "That's the reason I asked Mr. Davenport to bring you boys down here today." She nodded at Noah. "First of all, I told him about your app and he thought it would be a great invention to feature since it involves most of the students."

Noah beamed even more than I thought was possible.

She turned to me. "And you, Tom Swift. I wanted you here because . . . well it's the *Swift* Academy, after all!"

I felt a bowling ball settle in my stomach. A while back, I was at the center of a news piece on the academy (at least at first), and I wasn't so thrilled about it. It was the worst thing that could happen to someone who just wanted to blend in with the rest of the students. The thought of a camera crew following me around seemed like that first interview on steroids.

My half-smile was getting a real workout today. "Great," I said with a nervous laugh.

2

The Innovative Invasion

"DUDE, DID YOU HEAR THAT?" NOAH ASKED AS
we walked back to class. "We're going to be famous!"

I nodded. "I heard. I was there, remember?"

Noah stepped in front of me and stopped. "Come on.
Tell me you're not excited about this. Not even a little?"

I shrugged. "I don't really watch reality shows."

"Yeah, but now you'll get to *be* on one," Noah explained.

"Yeah," I agreed. "It looks that way."

Noah rolled his eyes. "Aw, man. This isn't your thing
about not wanting any special treatment, is it?"

Being my best friend, Noah knew all too well how

16

I felt about being called out because of my name or because of my father. He didn't necessarily agree with my reasoning. In fact, many times he'd tell me how he'd gladly trade places with me.

I rubbed the back of my neck. "Yeah, I guess it is. You know I don't like being in the spotlight when I haven't earned it."

"Well, don't worry about that," Noah said with a dismissive wave. "You heard what Ms. Jensen said. They want to feature my new app. You'll still help me with that special filter for the camera, right?"

I nodded. "Of course." As we passed the gym, I saw something strange across the hall. "What's that?" I asked, only too happy to change the subject.

We walked over to a thin pink box mounted on the wall. A large red funnel was attached to the top and a sign with an arrow was mounted on the wall above the entire thing: CHEWING GUM RECEPTACLE. The triangular recycling logo was printed on the box.

"Whoa, we're recycling gum now?" I asked. The academy had always been big on recycling, but this was a new one for me.

Noah wrinkled his nose. "That's all kinds of nasty.

I feel sorry for Mr. Jacobs having to empty that thing."

"No kidding," I agreed.

Mr. Jacobs was the school custodian. A while back, a few of us had to help him with his custodial duties. It gave me a new respect for his job of cleaning up after an entire school of messy students.

Noah and I made our way to our first class and quietly stepped inside. We handed Mr. Jenkins our tardy slips and took our seats. Luckily, he was in the middle of going over our algebra homework, so we hadn't really missed anything. Several completed math problems were projected on the screen at the front of the classroom.

While he helped a student across the room, I felt a tap on my shoulder and then heard a familiar voice in my ear. "All right, Swift," Sam whispered. "What have you two been up to?"

Noah and I spun in our seats to face our good friends Samantha Watson and Amy Hsu.

"Check it," Noah whispered. "They're going to make a reality show here!"

"What?" Sam asked. She peered over her glasses,

looking skeptical. "That doesn't make any sense."

When she glanced at me for confirmation, I nodded. "It's true."

Amy wrung her hands and lowered her head. Her long dark hair obscured part of her face, her occasional shield against the outside world. "They're going to film us? All of us?"

It turned out that Noah didn't have to explain further. At that very moment, Mr. Davenport's voice sounded over the intercom system. "Pardon the interruption, faculty and students," he said. "I have a few brief announcements. First of all, beginning tomorrow, a small crew will be here filming a new reality program based on our academy's students."

A murmur of excitement rippled through our classroom. I imagined similar scenes happening throughout the rest of the school. Noah grinned and nodded at Sam and Amy in a *What did I tell you?* sort of way.

"I'm *told* that the crew won't be disruptive and, after a few days, we won't even realize they're there," Mr. Davenport continued. "Either way, your last-period classes will have release forms for you to take home and have your parents sign. If you don't want to be on the show, I'm told that the production will blur your face or something similar."

Amy's shoulders relaxed a bit. She sighed and pulled her hair away from her face. I couldn't imagine Amy, one of the shiest people I knew, wanting to be on a television show of any kind.

"Not only will this be great publicity for the academy," Mr. Davenport continued, "but I've been told the production company is donating a state-of-the-art editing suite to the school. They'll be using the equipment to edit the show on-site, and once production is complete, they've generously agreed to provide it for student use."

Amy smiled, no longer self-conscious at all. The three of us knew about Amy's small collection of short films and animations. Actually, I think we were the only ones who knew about them. Her meticulous nature and near-perfect internal clock helped make her a talented editor and animator.

"Do you think they'll let students help with the editing?" she asked.

I shrugged. "I have no idea. Maybe."

"My second brief announcement is about this month's invention convention," Mr. Davenport said.

"As another public relations opportunity, we're going to expand it into a public event called the Inventors' Olympics."

More murmurs broke out in the classroom as Mr. Davenport went on to explain the event. The class seemed to be split between excitement and slight anxiety. It was one thing to show off a new invention in front of your fellow students, but the pressure was dialed up when you knew it was going to be seen by the public. I hadn't planned on showcasing anything in the upcoming convention—it was difficult to show an audience my cool glasses unless I made a pair for everyone. Still, I imagined I'd be a bit anxious if I did have something planned.

"And finally . . ." Mr. Davenport let out a breath. "I've been asked to instruct everyone to dispose of his or her used chewing gum in one of the receptacles you'll find in the hallways. This is part of a recycling invention created by our very own Miss Amy Hsu. Thank you for your time, everyone."

My eyes widened. Amy was behind the gum thing? I glanced back at her, but she was already hunched forward in her seat, scrolling through the digital textbook on her tablet. Her hair curtains cut her off from the rest of the class's gawking.

"No way," Noah said. He glanced at Sam. "You knew about this?"

Sam didn't get a chance to answer. "All right, everyone," Mr. Jenkins said. "Let's get back to it, shall we?"

That temporarily cut off the chatter about the film crew within our group, as well as the rest of the class. Even so, for the rest of the morning, the entire school was buzzing about the news. As expected, some students were apprehensive, but most were excited about being part of both the Inventors' Olympics *and* a new reality show.

"I bet someone will see my invention and want to buy it," Evan Wittman said during second period.

"Maybe I can be on *Squatch Hunters* after this," I heard Ashley Robbins say during third period. "I love that show!"

Noah must have spread the word about what other reality shows the producers had created. Let me tell you, if you ever want to spread news, modes of communication include the telegraph, telephone, and tell Noah.

When the "formidable foursome" (as my dad likes to call us) sat down for lunch together, we were not immune to the day's trending topics.

"It's *so* not real," Sam said as she plopped her lunch bag onto the table.

Noah set his tray down and pulled out a seat. "It's right there in the name . . . *reality* television."

"Don't you think if the squatch hunters ever found Bigfoot it would be all over the news?" Sam asked. "It would blow up the Internet."

Noah waved her away before pulling out a sandwich. "Whatever."

Amy twirled her fork through her salad, not taking a bite. "But do we have to be on the show if we don't want to be?"

I shook my head. "You heard Mr. Davenport. If your parents don't sign the release form, then you won't be on the show."

Sam pointed a fork at her. "You'll just have a blurry face, like you're in witness protection or something."

Amy sighed, relieved. "That's fine with me."

Noah popped a grape into his mouth. "There's something much bigger to worry about, though," he said between bites. "Since Davenport announced the show, that's all everyone's been talking about. I've hardly seen anyone using my app. There's no way everybody's collected enough loot to feed the beast today."

My best friend had a point. Since he'd launched his app, more and more of our classmates had been scanning the hallways looking for cartoon food items to use at the end of the school day. But since the announcement, I couldn't remember seeing anyone using the app between classes. After glancing around, I only spotted a couple of students in the cafeteria searching the room for loot.

"Maybe you should just lower the amount of food it takes to satisfy the beast," Sam suggested.

Noah shook his head. "That defeats the purpose of the game. Everyone is supposed to work together, tell their friends, get more and more people to participate."

Sam rolled her eyes. "I think you'll survive."

"Yeah, but Ms. Jensen said the producers wanted to feature my app," Noah explained. He jutted a thumb toward me. "Tom's even going to build a special lens to help."

"That's true." I explained how I planned to use the technology of my glasses so the cameras could pick up the loot *and* the beast.

"You can have Mr. Davenport make a special announcement," Amy suggested. "Like I did."

"Oh yeah." I rounded on Amy. "I didn't know you were behind the gum thing."

"I did," Sam said with a smug grin.

"How in any known universe is *that* your project?" Noah asked. "Especially for a germaphobe like you."

Noah had a point. I wouldn't necessarily describe Amy as a germaphobe, but she has always been a little more than obsessed with cleanliness. In fact, in her backpack (which is so well-equipped, it would put Batman's utility belt to shame), there were bound to be at least two bottles of hand sanitizer.

Amy laughed. "I almost didn't go through with the project, but my parents talked me into it. They said it was good to move out of my comfort zone once in a while. That's how we grow."

I sighed and nodded. "Yeah, my dad says the same thing." That's the same logic he'd used to get me to agree to that interview a while back.

"How do you recycle gum, anyway?" Noah asked. "Isn't it from a tree or a root or something?"

Amy's eyes lit up. "It used to be, but now most of it's made from a synthetic rubber."

"You know, like car tires," Sam added.

Noah's mouth dropped open. "I don't think I want to chew gum anymore."

"This wasn't my original idea," Amy continued. "There are already people installing gum receptacles in Europe. But I wanted to come up with a system that students could do themselves, maybe set it up in their own schools and use the recycled product for their 3-D printers or something."

Amy is usually soft-spoken, but when you get her going about one of her inventions, she can't be stopped.

"If all goes well, I'm going to be collaborating with Sam," she continued with a wide grin. "Give her the raw material for *her* invention."

"Which is?" I asked, turning to face Sam.

She took a bite of her pasta and shook her head. "I'm not saying yet."

Noah rolled his eyes. "Whatever it is, I still say messing with used chewing gum is all kinds of nasty."

• • •

Throughout the rest of the afternoon, I tried to put the reality show and upcoming Olympics out of my head. I think I wasn't the only one, since I heard less and less chatter about becoming TV stars *and* I saw more and more students hunting for loot with Noah's app. Maybe today would be the day that we satisfied the beast after all.

When the final bell rang, I gathered my belongings as quickly as possible and met Noah outside. Just as the days before, we weren't the only ones waiting on the school's front lawn after classes. Dozens of students faced west, holding their phones out in front of them.

"About the same as yesterday," Noah said as he glanced around. "I don't think it'll be enough."

"You never know," I said. "Maybe a couple of them found most of the loot."

Noah shrugged. "Maybe." He held up his phone. "We're about to find out."

I did the same, aiming my phone's camera in the same direction as everyone else. At first, I just saw the modest skyline of Shopton. But as always, I felt it before I saw anything. My phone began vibrating in my hand, though it wasn't as strong as when someone was calling. There were just little bursts in a slow, repeating pattern, simulating the beast's footsteps as it approached.

I focused on the screen, examining the skyline, and then I spotted it. A small figure appeared on the horizon, but it quickly grew in size as it lumbered forward.

Around us, other students were pointing at the horizon and scanning the skyline with their phones. It didn't take long before everyone was angling their phones identically like the panels of a solar farm.

Through my screen, the figure grew larger, until it resolved into a giant reptilian monster. Of course, there wasn't *really* an enormous beast trundling through Shopton. Noah did a fantastic job blending the animated creature in with the surroundings, making its feet disappear behind trees and buildings so it looked like it was really there . . . as long as you were looking at your screen. If he'd been sloppier, the beast might've just looked like a goofy cartoon.

As the beast moved closer, more detail came into focus. This wasn't your typical reptilian monster like a giant dinosaur or Godzilla. Noah had designed a cyborg. One of the creature's meaty arms had been replaced with a robotic appendage with a buzz saw at the end; electricity rippled over the metal blades running down its back, and one of its eyes was a red laser. You could see its thin beam sweep the area as the beast turned its head.

With the beast's next shuddering step, a cartoon barrel flew into frame, arcing toward the creature. Someone had launched one of their collected food items.

"Aw, too soon," Noah said. "They have to wait until it gets closer."

Noah had programmed the game with semirealistic physics. That meant the beast had to be close enough for the launched food to actually reach its mouth. Nevertheless, there was always someone who jumped the gun.

My phone trembled with more powerful vibrations as the beast stomped closer. In just a few more steps it would loom over the school.

"Now!" Noah shouted.

I tapped the app's big red Launch button and one of my items shot into frame. A cartoon turkey leg tumbled through the air toward the beast's open mouth. On my screen, I could see other items hurtling on the same trajectory. As my turkey leg entered the creature's mouth, points were added to my score. I kept tapping until all of my collected loot had disappeared down the creature's gullet.

In no time, the streams of cartoon food slowed and then stopped as everyone ran through their inventory. The beast let out a large belch (my phone really vibrated on that one) and then continued toward the school.

Noah shook his head. "Yeah, I didn't think that would be enough."

The creature brought down its buzz-saw arm on the roof, and sparks flew as a chunk of the school fell away. Noah had done such a great job with the animation that I caught myself glancing past my phone to make sure that the school was still intact.

Noah turned to me and grinned. "Wait until you see what I added for this one."

I turned my attention back to the screen and spotted four tiny figures stepping out onto the roof. Even though they were cartoon versions, I recognized their uniforms and gear immediately. The four original Ghostbusters readied their proton packs and blasted the beast with four gyrating orange streams of light.

"Cool," I said with a laugh. I heard other students join in around me.

Not so cool for the cartoon Ghostbusters, though. The beast reached down with its flesh hand and scooped them up, then popped them into its mouth in one fluid motion. More laughter and a few gasps echoed around us.

"Amy helped me with the animation on that one," Noah explained.

The rest of the animation continued as it had before: the beast sliced, punched, smashed, and stomped at the building until there was nothing left. Then it turned and slowly ambled back the way it had come.

As the crowd began to disperse, the high score flashed across the screen. Evan Wittman had successfully collected and launched the most food items—again.

3

The Culinary Calamity

THAT EVENING AFTER I FINISHED MY HOMEWORK, I tested yet another augmented reality invention. Okay, it wasn't a cool app like Noah's. Not *that* kind of augmented reality. Instead, I was going to cook dinner— virtually. Using robot arms I'd built in robotics class and the body of one of our early battlebots, I'd created a kind of virtual chef that I could operate remotely.

My creation was just a prototype, so it didn't look pretty. Picture a gear-covered stick man mounted to the top of an automated vacuum cleaner. A large pipe rose out of its mobile base with a camera mounted at the top.

Just below the camera, I'd fitted two shorter pipes perpendicularly and attached my robotic arms to the end of each. The entire thing was covered in gears, pulleys, and belts that enabled the arms to move and gave them leverage.

I wanted to surprise my dad with my latest creation, but I didn't know how I was going to do it since it took a while to assemble in the kitchen. Luckily, he'd been working in his home office since we got home.

Since my mother died a few years ago, my father has tried to be two parents in one and limit work to the office, but running a high-tech company like Swift Enterprises doesn't always allow him to do that. Sometimes, he has to bring work home. Tonight's session had given me time to set up my big unveiling.

I heard Dad's home office door open and footsteps coming down the stairs. "Something smells good," he said. "Thanks for cooking tonight. It's a tremendous help . . ." His voice trailed off as he saw me standing in the middle of the living room.

See, my father knew that if I was cooking dinner, it would be just one thing, pancakes—pretty much the only thing I like to cook. What he didn't expect was to see me doing it from another part of the house. The camera transmitted the scene from the kitchen to my special glasses. I was using the controllers from my augmented reality game to operate the robot arms.

"I thought you were cooking dinner," Dad said.

"I am," I replied without looking at him. "Go check it out."

He edged around me and made his way to the kitchen. I carefully flipped one of the pancakes before rotating the robot ninety degrees. The camera transmitted the image of my father standing in the kitchen doorway. I slowly waved the robot arm, the one holding the spatula with its claw.

A grin stretched across Dad's face. "Hey, that's nice."

"Thanks," I replied, turning the robot back to face the griddle.

Now I don't know if it was the urge to show off in front of my dad, or if I was just overconfident, but I tried something I hadn't done before: I poured pancake batter with my left robot arm while simultaneously removing a cooked pancake with my right. And then I wished I hadn't. I tilted the plastic pitcher in my left claw too far, spilling batter onto the floor.

"Uh-oh," I muttered as I instinctively jerked my left arm. Even more goo sloshed out of the pitcher. I tried to back the robot base away from the mess, but the treads spun and slipped in the batter. Before I knew it, my view of the kitchen radically changed as my robot toppled to the ground.

"Oh man," I said as I pulled off my glasses and dropped the controllers. I ran to the kitchen to see the mess I'd made in person. My father stood there shaking his head, a glob of pancake batter splashed across his shirt and pants.

"What's that you always say?" I asked with half a smile. "Back to the drawing board?"

My father chuckled as he grabbed a kitchen towel and wiped at the batter on his shirt. "It would seem so."

As my dad went upstairs to change, I cleaned up the mess. There was just enough un-spilled batter left for me to finish cooking dinner—the old-fashioned way.

I was flipping the last pancake as Dad came back downstairs. He poked his head around the corner of the dining room. "Is it safe to come in now?"

I laughed as I placed the not-so-tall stack of pancakes on the table. "Yeah. And sorry about that."

My father waved away my apology. "These things happen," he said as he took his seat. "Failure is all part of learning and moving forward."

That was the cool thing about being a second-generation inventor. My father was very understanding when one of my projects went haywire. He has told me plenty of times that he wouldn't be where he was today if he hadn't learned from the occasional failed invention.

As we ate, I explained my robot design, and he helped me troubleshoot what could've gone wrong. As always, he had some great suggestions on how to tighten up the robot's movements.

"Are you going to show off your robot in the upcoming Olympics?" he asked.

"You heard about that, huh?" I asked between bites.

"Of course," my dad said. "Holly Jensen works for me, after all. Plus, she was very excited to tell me about both of her ideas."

"The reality show thing?" I asked. "You're okay with that?"

My father shrugged. "I don't see why not, as long as classes aren't disrupted, and I can't see Mr. Davenport letting that happen." He looked at me over the rims of his glasses. "Let me guess. . . . You're not so happy about it." He closed his eyes and put a finger to his temple. "I'm getting a vision," he said, swaying in his seat. "It's getting clearer. . . . You're—you're worried about being the focus of that show because of your name."

I rolled my eyes. "How did you guess?"

"Oh, I've heard this story before," he replied. "Look, Tom. You can't change who you are. But have you ever thought that the harder you try to make things *not* about you, the more you're making things *all* about you?"

I opened my mouth to object but caught myself. My dad had a point. Maybe I was making too big a deal out of the whole attention thing. If the other kids at school wanted to be a part of a new reality show, why should I grumble about it?

"You're probably right," I finally said. "I know that Noah is sick of hearing me complain about not wanting special treatment. He always says he wouldn't feel the same way if it were him in my place."

My dad pointed his fork at me. "There you go. Maybe this show will give him a turn to be in the spotlight."

"Oh yeah," I said with a smile. "I think it will." Then

I told Dad about how Ms. Jensen wanted to feature Noah's augmented reality app.

"Sounds good to me. From what you've told me, his app brings the whole school together, involving everyone." He finished his last bite of pancake. "As far as I'm concerned, that's what the Swift Academy is all about."

4

The Production
Introduction

THE NEXT DAY AT SCHOOL, THE SWIFT ACADEMY students were all about getting on camera. As I entered through the front doors, I saw tons of students crowded around, chattering excitedly. Moving closer, I could make out a young man and woman, each with a video camera, recording the mob. Two other men held large microphones over the assembled students, and another man with a thick beard pointed at different people, instructing the camera operators where to shoot. Meanwhile, my classmates were mugging for the cameras. From my angle, it looked more like a zombie movie than a reality show.

I edged away from the group, making my way toward my locker.

"All right, people," Mr. Davenport said as he squeezed through the crowd. "Time to go to class." His face and bald head were flushed with anger.

His instruction was answered with moans of disappointment, but even so, the students quickly dispersed.

"Mr. Stewart," said Mr. Davenport as he approached the bearded man. "I was assured this wasn't going to be a disruption."

Mr. Stewart chuckled. "Please call me Joey. This always happens at first. The kids needed to get it out of their systems, and we'll be able to use the footage down the line."

"Okay . . . Joey," said Mr. Davenport. "I'm trying to run a school here and—"

Joey Stewart put a hand on the principal's shoulder. "Ronald . . . Ron. Can I call you Ron?" He didn't wait for a reply. "How about Sean and I go back to your office and get some shots of you at your desk." He held out his other hand, fingers spread wide. "The captain at the helm, that sort of thing."

Mr. Davenport nervously ran a hand over what little hair he had left. "Well, I suppose that would be all right."

"Good," Joey said as he led the man away from the group. "We'll make an announcement too, so this won't happen again." The male camera operator and one of the mic guys followed the pair as they moved toward the main office.

As I dialed in the combination to my locker, Noah slid up beside me. "How cool was that?"

"Pretty cool, I guess. It kind of looked like a flash mob."

Noah laughed. "Yeah. I think I got on camera a couple of times!" He brushed imaginary debris from one of his shoulders. "I'm going to be a star."

I pulled a folder out of my locker and waved it in front of him. "Then you won't have to worry about your algebra assignment. I'm sure your folks will be so proud."

Noah's eyes went wide. "Uh . . . see you in class." I laughed as my best friend darted through the busy hallway, trying to get to his locker.

When I walked into class, Amy and Sam were already there. I guess they hadn't been caught up in the reality TV traffic jam.

I slid into my seat and spun to face my friends. "Did you see the big . . ." My voice trailed off when I saw Amy. Her lips were pressed into a thin line and she was fidgeting her hands more than usual.

"Amy's parents signed the release form and made her promise to give the show a try," Sam explained.

Amy took in a deep breath, then sighed it out. "They didn't exactly *make* me promise," she said. "You remember that 'get out of my comfort zone' thing I mentioned?"

"Yeah?" I tilted my head.

"This TV thing falls into that category."

Sam rolled her eyes.

"It'll be fine, Amy," I said, trying to sound reassuring. "From what I saw, a lot of students are trying to get on camera. Maybe you can just blend into the background."

"You think so?" Amy asked, perking up a little.

Sam's eyes widened. "You could make a game of it. See a camera, keep your head down."

Amy shrugged and a small smile pulled at her lips. "I kind of do that anyway."

Sam and I laughed, and Amy joined in.

Just then, Noah rushed into the classroom and slid into his seat. The bell rang a moment after he hit the chair. Amy must have been really upset, otherwise, her near-perfect internal clock would have let us know he was about to be tardy.

Noah waved a folder triumphantly. "That's right." His brow wrinkled when he saw our smiles. "What did I miss?"

None of us had the chance to answer before Mr. Jenkins rose from his desk and moved to the smartboard. "All right, sports fans. If you'll pull out yesterday's assignments—"

"Pardon the interruption, faculty and students," came Mr. Davenport's voice over the intercom system.

Mr. Jenkins sighed and returned to his desk.

"After this morning's . . . introduction to the camera crew," our principal continued, "I think it's best we lay down some ground rules."

"Maybe it'd be better if you let me explain," said another voice in the background.

"Oh, uh . . . okay," said Mr. Davenport.

There was some shuffling. "Hello, Swift Academy students," said the second voice, much louder this time. "My name is Joey Stewart, and I'm the producer for this little program we'll be shooting at your school."

All the kids in Mr. Jenkins's class glanced around the room, grinning. It seemed that everyone except Amy, Sam, and I was thrilled with the idea of being on television.

"Now, we really enjoyed the warm welcome this morning, and we got a lot of great footage," Mr. Stewart continued. "But from now on, it's extremely important that none of you look directly at any of the cameras. We can't use that kind of footage for the show."

Noah crossed his arms. "'Nuff said. There's no way they're gonna cut my footage."

The students closest to us snickered. Sam just rolled her eyes.

"I know it's going to be difficult," Mr. Stewart said, "but please try to ignore the crew while we're here. Thank you."

"All right, then," said Mr. Davenport. "You heard the man. Please continue your studies as usual."

When it was clear that the announcements were over, Mr. Jenkins stood once more, approaching the smartboard. "Okay, future reality stars. Let's get to those assignments, shall we?"

The classroom chatter faded and we went back to algebra as usual. I had almost completely forgotten about the camera crew when class ended. As we all filed out of the room, Mr. Stewart and Ms. Lane were waiting in the hallway. Luckily, none of the camera operators were around, so I didn't have to worry about where not to look.

Ms. Lane pointed first to Noah and then to me before walking away. Mr. Stewart marched toward us. "Ah! Noah and Tom, right?"

"That's us!" Noah said enthusiastically.

"Yes, sir," I replied.

The man shook our hands. "No *sir*s, and Mr. Stewart is my dad. Call me Joey."

"Okay, Joey," Noah said.

Joey crossed his arms and studied us. "Holly tells me that you two have an augmented reality app that has the whole school buzzing."

I pointed at my best friend. "Actually, it's Noah's app."

"Right," Joey replied, "but you're the one who's going to help our camera see everything, right?"

With everything going on, I had completely forgotten about agreeing to build the special lens filter. "Uh, yeah. But I haven't built it yet."

Joey moved between us and put a hand on each of

our shoulders. "No worries. Plenty of time for that." He guided us down the hallway. "While I've got you boys, let me show you your school's new editing suite."

"Uh, we're going to be late for class," I said.

Joey grinned and reached into his back pocket. "No worries on that, either." He pulled out a small pink pad. "Your principal gave me a bunch of signed hall passes."

"Cool," Noah said.

I could see the wheels turning in my friend's mind. If the academy had a black market, that pad would be worth a fortune.

We followed Joey up to the second floor to the workroom next to the computer lab. Normally, the room stored several components and spare computer parts. Now, however, the place looked like a gamer's paradise. A huge workstation was set up on one end of the room with not one, but three, computer monitors. And a giant flat-screen television was mounted on the wall above it all. The computer screens were filled with the virtual dials and knobs of a professional editing software package. A thin man with glasses sat at the workstation while a video clip of the crowd of students from earlier played on the large TV screen.

"This is Danny, our editor," Joey said as we entered the room. "He's going to be editing our show on-site, as we film it."

Danny didn't look up from the screens, but he raised a hand and waved.

"Whoa," Noah said. "This is sick!"

"Oh yeah," I agreed. I was with my friend on this one. If the reality show was going to donate this setup to the school, it might actually be worth it. "I can't wait to tell Amy about this."

"Who's Amy?" asked Joey.

"She's a friend of ours," replied Noah. "She's an excellent editor and animator."

"Is that right?" Joey put a hand on the editor's shoulder. This guy sure was the touchy-feely type. "Think you could use an assistant, Dan?"

Again, the editor didn't look up from his work. "It's what I've been telling you for three shows now."

Joey laughed, then moved toward the other end of the room. A thick black curtain had been hung to divide the space. He pulled the fabric back to reveal a small camera on a tripod flanked by two large lights. The camera was aimed at a folding chair positioned in front of a blue curtain. A large microphone was attached to a stand that boomed out over the chair.

"This is our confessional," Joey said.

I raised an eyebrow. "Confessional?"

"Oh yeah," Noah said. "It's where the people talk about what's happening on the show. I've seen that on a bunch of reality shows."

"There you go," Joey said. He turned to me and gestured toward the chair. "And I want you two to be the first to try it out."

I looked at Noah. He should really go first since he was the one who was excited about the show. I was about to say as much, but my best friend just grinned and nodded. I think he was giddy to see how a reality show worked.

I reluctantly took the seat in front of the lights, my stomach somersaulting with nerves.

Joey sat in a folding chair on the other side of the camera. "Okay, now I just want you to look into the camera lens and answer a few questions for me," Joey said. "Relax. No big deal."

I raised a finger. "I thought we weren't supposed to look at the cameras."

48

Joey waved away my concern. "That's just out there. In here, you *always* look into the camera."

I let out a long breath, trying to settle my stomach. "Okay."

Joey pressed a button and a small red light blinked above the lens. "All right, Tom Swift . . . how does it feel to share a name with your school?"

So much for avoiding special treatment.

I glanced up at Noah for help, but my best friend simply nodded back at me with that same big stupid grin on his face.

5

The Disputation Observation

"ALL RIGHT," JOEY SAID. "LAST QUESTION . . .
What are some of the inventions that you're most
proud of?"

I breathed a little easier. He was finally asking a question that wasn't about my father, or the Swift Academy,
or what it was like being the son of the man who created the entire school. I was so surprised by this turn in
the interview that my mind went blank for a moment.

"Oh, uh—" I stammered. "There's the—oh yeah. I
invented an alarm clock where you have to answer different math equations before the alarm shuts off."

Joey nodded. "Interesting . . ."

"Tell him about our cloud seeding project," Noah chimed in.

"That's right," I said, sitting up straighter. "Noah and I actually made it rain using model rockets." I went on to explain how each rocket had shot into a low cloud and dumped a payload of chemicals that made water droplets form. People had been doing that for years, but Noah and I created the same effect with a dozen two-stage model rockets.

"That's great," Joey said. "But aren't you forgetting something?" He tapped his temple with his index finger.

I cocked my head, trying to figure out what he meant. But then I reached up and felt the pair of augmented reality glasses resting on my forehead. My face warmed as I let out a long sigh. I can't believe I had them on my head the entire time. I must've looked like such a nerd.

I pulled the glasses off my head. "These special glasses let me see elements of Noah's augmented reality app without using my phone."

Joey grinned. "Excellent."

"Uh, and they also let me operate this rudimentary robot I created," I quickly added. "I can see what it sees and operate its hands using the controllers from my console."

Joey reached over and paused the camera. "I think that's all we need for now." He pulled out the pad of hall passes, tore off the top sheet, and handed it to me. "Let's give Noah a turn."

"Yeah, okay," I said as I got to my feet. I had to admit, I was a little disappointed. The questions were just getting interesting.

I moved out of the way so Noah could take the seat in front of the camera. He patted down his hair, looking at his reflection in the lens. I wish I had thought of that. If I had, I might've noticed the glasses sitting on my head.

"Want me to stick around?" I asked. Maybe I could jog Noah's memory the way he'd helped with mine.

"That's all right," Joey answered. "I don't want to keep you from class any longer than necessary." He gave a quick wink. "I might get in trouble again with your principal."

"Oh . . . all right," I said as I pulled the curtain aside. "I'll see you later," I told Noah.

"Yeah, man," Noah replied without looking up. He continued to check his reflection.

I left the editing suite feeling relieved the encounter was over, but oddly unwelcome at the same time. It was weird. I'd never felt so subtly dismissed before.

I swung by my locker and then headed toward my second-period class. Luckily, Joey's hall pass did the trick.

Noah didn't show up for the rest of the period. And even though I didn't have every class with him, I didn't spot him in the halls for the rest of the morning. Joey must've kept him busy showing off his augmented reality app.

I was happy for my friend. After all, he seemed to be the most excited about being on television. But I was also worried about him. I hoped that all the time on the show wouldn't affect his schoolwork. Then again, we'd worked on side projects and special inventions that took our attention away from our homework a bunch of times. The thought came to mind because it was one of those things my father warned me about repeatedly: spreading myself too thin. In the end, we always caught up. Neither Noah nor I were ever going to be in the running for top of the class, but we always managed to keep our grades up no matter what else we had going on.

Come lunchtime, Noah was still a no-show. That surprised me a little, but not as much as Sam and Amy being AWOL too. The four of us almost always had lunch together.

With a sigh, I settled at a table by myself. At least I could use the time to work on my designs for the lens filter they wanted me to create for the show.

I pulled out my notebook from my backpack. The worn spiral book held most of my invention ideas, and I took it everywhere. You never knew when or where inspiration would strike. Sure, I could type notes on my phone if I had to, but I always felt more creative writing in my notebook, maybe sketching out a crude drawing or two while everything was fresh in my mind.

I found a blank page and began scribbling some ideas for the filter. I would need a clear piece of glass as well as a small video screen to reflect the image onto the glass, just as I had done with my glasses. I drew a square to represent the piece of glass and then began sketching out adjustable mounting brackets that could be attached to the camera lens. The brackets had to be adjustable so the glass could move closer or farther away to bring the projected image into focus.

I was so engrossed in my design that I didn't notice when Sam approached my table. I hate to admit it, but I jumped when I saw her from the corner of my eye.

"Easy there, Swift," she said, her voice a bit muffled.

Sam's voice was muffled because she was wearing a transparent full-face shield, along with a pair of rubber gloves. She held a plastic bucket in one hand and a metal paint scraper in the other.

"What's with all the"—I pointed at her weird accessories—"everything?"

"I'm helping out Amy with her project," Sam said. "With the upcoming Olympics and all, her gum receptacles aren't filling as fast as she'd like." She let out a sigh. "We're moving on to plan B."

"What's plan . . ." I started to ask as Sam dropped to her knees and crawled under the table. "Oh no," I said.

"Oh yes," Sam said as she began to scrape the underside of the table.

I scooted back in my chair to give her more room. "That's . . . disgusting."

"You get used to it," Sam said as a thick wad of gum plopped into the bucket. "The library was worse."

I shook my head. "You're a really, *really* good friend.

I'm sure Amy's germaphobia would be on overload if she had to do this herself."

"Nah," Sam said between scrapes. "I offered to do it all, but she wouldn't hear it."

"No way," I said.

That's when I heard an eruption of laughter. I turned to see another bucket-wielding figure enter the cafeteria. If I didn't know it was Amy, I wouldn't have recognized her. She was covered from head to toe in a plastic hazmat suit. She wore rubber gloves and a face shield like Sam, but Amy also had a cloth surgical mask stretched over her mouth and nose. Her eyes were the only part of her body that was visible, and they were behind a pair of safety goggles *under* the clear face shield. She looked as if she wasn't taking any chances. For someone who wanted nothing more than to blend into the background, Amy was now the center of attention. But if I knew Amy, being completely covered gave her more confidence, even if it meant being more visible.

Amy gave me a nervous wave with her scraper before shuffling over to an unoccupied table. The laughter soon died down as she crawled underneath and got to work.

That was one of the interesting things about our

school: seeing someone in protective gear wasn't an unusual occurrence.

There was a little time left in lunch period, so I was about to offer to help, but I quickly changed my mind when I noticed one of the camera operators enter the cafeteria. My table was closest to the door, so the cameraman made a beeline for it. As casually as I could, I packed up my stuff, grabbed my tray, and moved toward the kitchen. Luckily, a kid with a lunch tray wasn't as interesting as someone in safety gear working under a table. The operator crouched and steadied the camera, getting a shot of Sam at work.

I swung by my locker and then made it to robotics class just in time. Of course, Noah was a no-show again. I guessed Sam would be late since she had to get out of all that gear. Luckily, our robotics teacher, Mrs. Scott, was pretty lenient as long as you didn't fall behind in your work.

I had already brought in my robot and stowed it in the storeroom. I grabbed it and placed it on one of the large worktables. Turning it on its side, I worked at taking apart the base. I wasn't looking forward to cleaning out dried pancake batter from the treads and gears down there.

I was almost finished when Noah finally breezed into class. Unfortunately, he wasn't alone; one of the camera crews was right behind him. A short brown-haired woman held the camera, and a tall balding man held the boom mic. They broke off from Noah and began recording some of the other students working on their projects. I saw Jamal Watts stiffen a little when they showed an interest in his work. As instructed, he didn't look at the camera and did his best to ignore his new audience.

"Long time no see," I said to Noah as he dropped his backpack onto our worktable.

Noah grinned. "Yeah, I took Lori and Pete around the school, showing them all the hidden loot in my app." He held up his phone. "There's a lot of stuff left today, though. I don't think as many people are playing as before."

I nodded toward the camera crew. "I guess everyone is distracted by the filming."

Noah shook his head. "If this keeps up, we'll never collect enough loot to feed the beast." He ran a hand over his head. "Maybe I should get Davenport to make an announcement, like he did for Ames."

"That's a good idea," I agreed as I cleaned out the last bit of debris from my robot's gears. I grabbed a screwdriver and began to reassemble the base.

Noah pulled a stool close to mine and sat down. "So how's the lens filter coming? I had to hold my phone up in front of the camera today. You could see the loot, but the image wasn't that great."

"Oh yeah." I dropped the screwdriver onto the table and pulled my notebook from my backpack, opened it, and thumbed through the pages. "I have the lens all figured out." Once I found the correct page, I pointed at my design.

Noah leaned over my sketch. "This is all you've got?" he asked. "You haven't even started building it yet?"

"Uh, there's this little thing you might've noticed called school."

Noah pointed to my robot. "You have time to work on your project, though."

I felt my face flush with anger. "One, you know this is a school assignment. And two, why should your project be more important than anyone else's?"

"Because it is," Noah said stretching his arms wide. "You know they're going to feature it on the show."

"Oh yeah," I said with an eye-roll. "I forgot all about the *Noah Newton Show*."

Noah put a hand to his ear. "Is that jealousy I hear? For once, everything isn't about Tom Swift?"

I couldn't believe what he was saying. Of all people, Noah knew that I didn't like special treatment. Heck, he was usually the one making fun of me for wanting out of the spotlight.

My lips pressed together as I pushed the notebook toward him. "Why don't you build it yourself, then?"

"Because you said you'd do it." Noah pushed the notebook back to me.

"Fine. If it'll shut you up." I shoved away from the worktable and got to my feet.

I'd planned to go to the storage room to get the parts I needed for the lens brackets. Instead, I froze in my tracks. Everyone in the class was staring at us. Worse, the camera crew was a couple of feet away.

And they had recorded our entire argument.

6

The Dissension Impression

I DIDN'T SPEAK TO NOAH FOR THE REST OF THE day. Or for the entire next day, for that matter. It felt weird being so angry with my best friend, but I couldn't stop thinking about what he had said. He was always razzing me about not wanting to be the center of attention, but this time was definitely over the line.

I wondered if he knew that the camera had been on us. That would explain why he went there during our argument, but it certainly didn't excuse it. Honestly, the thought of that possibly being Noah's motivation made me even angrier.

Sam had tried to smooth things over between us before algebra. Of course, it was in her Sam-like way. "Look at you two," she'd said. "Did you suddenly get sent back to third grade and no one told us?"

Yeah, that hadn't worked at all.

Amy, on the other hand, had just sat there looking uncomfortable. She really hated any kind of conflict.

So Noah and I continued to give each other the silent treatment.

As for the camera crews, true to Joey's promise, everyone seemed to forget they were there. As I went about my day, I would see them following groups of students or simply planted in a hallway, catching students as they walked by. Out of the corner of my eye I even caught a camera recording me. Luckily, they didn't linger. I guess I wasn't doing anything interesting enough.

As the day went on, I noticed that Noah and I weren't the only ones on the outs. As I was walking to chemistry, I caught the tail end of an argument between Toby Nguyen and Ronny Jenkins.

"You totally stole my idea," Toby accused as they marched down the corridor.

"That's not true," Ronny replied. "My invention is

completely different. Besides, you said you were done with drones."

They moved out of earshot, so I couldn't make out what Toby said next, but I wondered if either of them had noticed that one of the camera crews was trailing along behind them.

They weren't the only people I saw bickering. Terry Stephenson and Evan Wittman were in a heated discussion in the back of the biology classroom. Even Barry Jacobs and Kaylee Jackson weren't speaking for some reason.

It was weird seeing so many people at odds with one another. Our school has always been about collaboration and teamwork. It's extremely rare that anyone would take someone's idea without asking. I could only think of one time when that happened, but luckily for Amy's sake, we were able to find out who had stolen her cool pop quiz app.

I'd also noticed that people in the halls were giving me strange looks. Maybe I was just being paranoid, but it seemed as if everyone was keeping an eye on me for some reason. Maybe word of Noah's and my dispute had gotten around and people were waiting to see how things played out. But it seemed that there was plenty of other people's drama to keep everyone entertained. I didn't know why I would be of particular interest.

Since Sam and Amy were still on chewing-gum detail, I took my lunch into the robotics classroom so I could finish building the lens filter for Noah's app. I wasn't doing it to get him off my back. (Okay, maybe that was one reason.) I had told him that I'd build the filter, and I wanted to keep my word. I certainly didn't want to give him any reason to think that I was trying to sabotage his big break.

Unpacking my notebook, I turned to the page with my filter designs. I'd also pulled out a tiny video screen that I'd brought from home after taking apart an old broken camcorder. Once the screen was mounted at just the right angle, it should be able to project an image onto the glass filter, working the same way my glasses did.

I was halfway through assembling the filter when Ms. Jensen walked into the classroom. "Ah, there you are, Tom," she said.

I put my tools down. "You're looking for me?"

"Yes, you're one of my last stops. I'd like to borrow any invention designs or blueprints you have."

I raised an eyebrow. "What do you mean?"

She clapped her hands together. "Well, since this school is chock-full of talented young inventors, I had the wonderful idea to use different blueprints as cool graphics during the show."

"I don't understand," I said. "You're working on the show too?"

Ms. Jensen gave a dismissive wave. "I like to pitch in where I can. Remember, eyes and ears everywhere or I wouldn't be good at my job."

"Oh, okay."

She pulled up a stool to my worktable. "Here's how it'll work: Say Joey records someone's invention in action. Well, before that, he'll cut to an animation of the blueprints in action. One of your fellow students, Amy Hsu, has even agreed to help with the animation."

"Oh yeah. She's great," I said. Amy had some mad animation skills, so if anyone could pull it off and make it look good, she could.

Still, I instinctively reached out and slid my notebook closer. "My designs are pretty crude, though," I said. "They're not what I'd call real blueprints."

Ms. Jensen glanced down at my sketch. "Oh, are these

them? May I?" She didn't wait for an answer before she picked up the notebook and began thumbing through the pages. "These are great. They'll be perfect."

It felt weird having a stranger look through my designs. Sure, there weren't any top-secret inventions like at my dad's company, but the notebook was filled with ideas that I hadn't fully fleshed out yet.

"I . . . I don't know," I said, slowly reaching out for my notebook.

"Oh, come on," she said. "Don't you want to help support your school? Besides, everyone else has been fine with it."

Yeah, but everyone else seems to have reality show fever, I thought.

Ms. Jensen clutched the notebook to her chest. "Please? We'll scan in the pages and get your plans back to you tomorrow."

I think the implied peer pressure finally won out. After all, were my inventions so special that they had to be more of a secret than anyone else's? If I didn't want anyone giving me special treatment based solely on my name, then I shouldn't give special treatment to myself, either, right? Still, I wasn't thrilled to just hand over my private notes. It wasn't like my notebook was a diary or anything, but for an inventor like me, it was almost just as personal.

I rubbed the back of my neck. "I . . . I guess so."

"Wonderful." Ms. Jensen got to her feet. "So glad you could help," she said, before she breezed out of the classroom with my notebook tucked under her arm.

I glanced down at my work and was tempted to run after her—she'd just walked off with my plans for the lens filter I was building. But I stopped myself when I realized that I no longer needed them. I'd already built all the components using the dimensions I'd written down. All that was left to do was the assembly, and the steps for that were in my head.

I sighed before going back to work. If I hurried, I could finish most of the filter before class began. Part of me wanted to get it out of the way so I could finish tweaking my robot. But a bigger part of me didn't want to work on the filter in front of Noah. I didn't want any suggestions from him and I didn't want to give him the satisfaction of seeing my attention focused on his project. It was petty, sure, but I was still angry about what he'd said.

As my classmates began filing in, I put away the last piece of the filter. It appeared I'd been worrying about Noah for nothing, since he was a no-show. In fact, I didn't see him again until everyone was gathered out front after school for the latest beast attack.

Just as Noah wanted, Mr. Davenport had made an announcement earlier reminding everyone about the app. The front grounds were packed with students holding their phones in front of them. Noah stood a few feet ahead and didn't turn around. Both camera crews were also set up recording the event.

"Did you download the update?" Sam asked as she moved in beside me.

I nodded. "Of course. Did Amy come up with another animation?"

Sam shrugged and gave a sly grin. "I'm not saying."

I shook my head and turned my attention back to my phone. The beast was just coming into view. As he moved into range, people began launching loot. Unfortunately, just as before, they didn't launch enough food to prevent an attack on the school. The beast stomped forward as Jacob Mahaley's name flashed across the screen. He was today's top loot collector.

This time there were no animated Ghostbusters to fend off the attack. Instead, a lone figure stood on the roof. He raised a bazooka and fired. The beast roared with frustration but kept coming. I held my phone higher and zoomed in on the figure, cracking up when I realized it was an animated Mr. Davenport. Amy had done a great job dressing him up in full military gear. I widened the image back out just in time to see the beast shake off another bazooka blast before biting down on the animated figure, swallowing him whole.

Everyone around me laughed, and Noah turned back to grin at me. He must've forgotten we were fighting for a moment. I just got out half a smile before his grin faded as he spun back around. So much for a truce.

7

The Association
Polarization

"AM I SUPPOSED TO BE SEEING SOMETHING YET?"
Lori, the camera operator, asked. She peered through
the eyepiece again.

I tightened one of the plastic zip ties holding my filter to her camera. "Not yet. We have to find some loot
for it to register."

I had finished the filter the night before and caught
up with one of the camera crews after second period.
Just as I had hoped, it didn't take much to attach the
device to the front of the camera. Pete, the sound guy,
had already downloaded Noah's app on his phone, so

it was no big deal to pair my filter with his phone via Bluetooth. It was the exact same way my glasses worked.

Unfortunately, there was no way to truly test the filter until we found one of the virtual food items hidden around the school. And since everyone was playing *Feed the Beast* with renewed vigor, those items would be hard to find.

"I think I know where we can find one," I said. "Follow me."

I led Lori and Pete down the nearby stairs and onto the second floor. We entered the chemistry lab and moved toward the nearby storeroom. We were between classes and Mrs. Gaines didn't seem to object. It appeared the teachers were getting used to the camera crews too.

When Noah had first created his app, he boasted to me about a few hard-to-find items he'd hidden throughout the school. One of them was sitting on a shelf among all the bottles and jars of various chemicals in the lab's storeroom. I just hoped it was hidden well enough to still be there.

I put my glasses on as I led the way through the door, then scanned the shelves until I spotted a cartoon bunch of bananas. "There," I told Lori as I pointed to them.

She aimed the camera toward the shelf and adjusted the lens. "I see something," she said. "A big, blurry, yellow something."

"Keep your eye on it," I said as I reached toward the camera. "I have to adjust the focus."

My special filter was a square piece of glass mounted on four rods, which were attached to a circular ring that went around the lens. Since I didn't know the exact size of the lens on each camera, I made the ring adjustable, and I'd attached it with zip ties. The key to my filter, however, was the small video screen mounted between the top two rods. The square glass was slightly angled away from the lens, and whatever came up on the tiny screen would be reflected on the glass. Even so, the distance between the screen and the glass had to be manually adjusted to bring the image into focus.

"Let me know when the image is sharp," I said as I carefully spun a tiny thumbscrew on the video mount.

"There," Lori said, and I pulled my hand away. She laughed. "That is *so* cool."

Just then, Maggie Ortiz poked her head in through the open doorway. She slowly raised her phone. She was getting ready to collect the loot.

"Maggie, wait a second," I said. "We're testing my new filter."

She lowered her phone and stepped inside. Meanwhile, Lori had her camera trained on the shelf as she recorded it from different angles. "Amazing," she said. "It's a little transparent, but it's like it's really there."

"The items won't look completely solid since they're projected onto the glass," I explained. "Just like with my glasses."

Lori lowered the camera and glanced back at Maggie. "Can I get a shot of you collecting the loot?"

Maggie beamed. "Sure!"

Lori directed Maggie where to stand so both she and the cartoon bananas would be in the shot. When Lori was ready, Maggie raised her phone to view the animated item herself. I watched through my glasses, so I could see the bananas fly off the shelf and zip over to Maggie's phone. The bunch of bananas shrunk at the last minute, making it appear to enter the phone itself. Maggie gave me a quick wave before exiting the storeroom.

"Very nice," Lori said as she lowered the camera from her shoulder. "Great job on this filter."

"Thanks."

"Now I just need to find more loot." Lori grinned.

"You can ask Noah," I suggested. "He knows where everything is hidden."

"Oh, sure," Lori said as she headed out. "He's been a big help all around."

I rolled my eyes. "I'm sure he has."

I followed Lori out of the rapidly filling lab and hustled to my locker. The bell rang just as I got there; I was already late for my next class. Lori had given me a hall pass, so I was okay on that front. I just needed to unload the tools I'd used for the filter from my backpack. It would be a lot lighter for the rest of the day. I'd noticed it felt especially light without my notebook.

I hadn't realized how much I would miss my constant companion. Most of my friends felt naked without their phones, but since Ms. Jensen had taken my notebook, everything had felt a little off. And sure, I had other notebooks at home filled with invention ideas, but my current one was like a part of me. I'd had to jot down the ideas and thoughts I had the night before on scraps of paper.

I'd head over to the editing suite at lunch. Ms. Jensen

should've had enough time to make sure all my designs had been scanned in by then.

When the bell for lunch rang, I hustled out of class to be the first in line. After grabbing my tray, I made my way to the editing suite. Dan was at the controls, cutting together segments for the show. On the main screen, I saw Jessica Mercer in a heated discussion with Mia Trevino. I didn't catch what they were going on about because my attention was grabbed by a new, smaller workstation off to the side. Amy sat in front of a computer, her lunch bag open beside her.

"Hey," I said as I pulled up a chair next to her. "You working through lunch too?"

Amy nodded as she swallowed and dabbed the corner of her mouth with a napkin. She reached across her desk and picked up my spiral notebook. "Looking for this?"

"Oh yeah," I replied as I reached out, trying to act casual and not at all like how I felt—a toddler reaching for his favorite toy.

Once my notebook was back in my hands, I let out a small sigh of relief. "You've scanned in everyone's invention plans?"

"Most everyone's," Amy replied. She reached over and patted a small portable hard drive. "The entire wisdom of Swift Academy is right here."

I wondered how much something like that would be worth. Sure, not every student came up with a million-dollar idea, but I bet there were plenty of cool innovations crammed onto that drive. Again, it was a good thing the academy didn't have a black market.

"What are you doing with the scans, exactly?" I asked.

Amy beamed with excitement. "Let me show you." Her fingers flew across the keyboard as she pulled up a list of file folders on her screen. Different students' names were printed beside each one. Amy scrolled through the list before selecting one labeled MILLS, JIM.

She opened the folder and then another file. Suddenly her screen was filled with a crude drawing of a two-seated vehicle that looked like a go-kart without wheels. Instead, enclosed fans were mounted to all four corners of the machine. A tubular roll cage was mounted over the seats.

"This is Jim's hovercraft," Amy explained.

I nodded and took a bite from an apple. "So that's what his roll cage was for."

A few weeks ago, a bunch of the students had partici-
pated in a lock-in at my father's company next door. I
remember that Jim had spent his time in the machine shop
a building a roll cage. He just didn't say what it was for. Of
course, after working on my project, burning circuit boards,
babysitting a junior reporter, and stopping some high-level
corporate espionage, I had forgotten all about Jim's project.

"And here's what I did," Amy said as she tapped a key
on the keyboard.

Suddenly, Jim's crude drawing sprang to life. The
four fans began to spin, and animated wind lines blew
through the blades. The craft lifted off the ground and
hovered there, slowly bouncing up and down.

"Wow, great job," I said. It seemed as if Amy's animation skills were getting better and better.

Amy grinned. "Thanks."

"She's quite the little animator," Dan added without
looking up from his work.

Amy blushed and stared at her lap.

"So what are you going to animate with my stuff?" I
quickly asked, hoping to get Amy to refocus.

She pulled up the list of folders again and scrolled
down to the one labeled SWIFT, TOM.

"I'm not sure yet," she said as she opened the folder and began to toggle through the scanned pages.

With all of my private sketches and designs displayed there for the world to see, my lunch suddenly didn't taste very good.

"Do you have an invention in mind?" Amy asked. "Something you're going to show off during the Olympics, maybe?"

"What?" I asked. "I mean . . ." I pointed to the glasses on my forehead. "My AR glasses, I guess."

Amy cocked her head. "I'm not sure what to animate there. What else do you have?"

"Oh, how about my robot?" I suggested. I explained how I could control it with my glasses and the controllers from my console. I told her about my cooking attempt. "It should be fine as long as I don't try to make pancakes for everyone."

Amy laughed. "That might work." She began clicking through the pages in my file.

"There," I said as she opened the page showing my rough sketch of my robot.

"Tom!" said a voice behind me. "Just the man I wanted to see."

I turned around as Joey entered the editing suite. "Oh, hi."

He clamped a hand on my shoulder. "We don't have enough confessional footage of you," he said. "You have time for another go?"

I glanced at my unfinished lunch tray. "Uh, sure . . . I guess so."

"Good, good," he said, ushering me toward the curtain separating that section of the editing suite.

"I'll see you later, Tom," Amy called as she gathered her lunch bag and headed out of the room.

Joey pulled back the curtain and I took a seat in front of the camera. The setup was the same as before: the camera pointing at me, the microphone hovering over my head. But one thing was different. A small video monitor was now mounted on a stand next to the camera.

Joey took a seat facing me and turned the camera on. He adjusted the angle and pressed the Record button. "So, Lori tells me the new lens filter works great. How did you create it?"

I took a deep breath and tried to act as casual as possible. "It uses the same principle as my glasses." I went on to explain how the tiny video monitor projected the image onto the glass.

"That sounds very exciting," Joey said. "Are you going to show off your glasses in the Inventors' Olympics?"

"Well, kind of," I replied. "I can also use them to control this robot I made. I think I'll showcase that somehow." I hoped Joey wouldn't ask me how, since I hadn't quite figured that part out yet.

He thoughtfully stroked his bushy beard. "So the glasses do more than just let you see the objects in Noah's app?"

"Oh yeah," I agreed with a small laugh. "Much more."

"What do you think about Noah getting so much attention for *Feed the Beast*?" Joey asked.

That was kind of a weird question. "It's fine, I guess." I shrugged.

Joey raised an eyebrow. "Really? Because I hear that you two aren't getting along lately."

I didn't understand why he wasn't asking me more about our inventions, but he was spot-on about the friction between Noah and me. Maybe Joey had seen the footage from our argument and was just curious.

"It's no big deal, really," I said, trying to play the situation off. "We just had a disagreement, that's all."

"You're not worried he's stealing the spotlight from you?"

"What spotlight?" I asked, annoyed. "I don't want any kind of spotlight."

"Hmm . . ." Joey nodded thoughtfully before pulling back the curtain and leaning out of the confessional. "Dan? Play us that clip we cued up." He pulled out a tiny notebook and flipped through the pages. "File: Newton eleven."

"Coming right up," came Dan's voice from the other side of the room.

Suddenly, the tiny video screen behind the confessional camera came to life. It showed an image of Noah sitting where I was now. He was staring at the camera with his mouth open, as if frozen in midsentence. After a few seconds, the video began to play.

"Get over yourself, Tom Swift. Just because your name's on the school doesn't mean that you're a big deal. You probably wouldn't be here if your dad hadn't built the school. You're not even that good of an inventor."

My jaw dropped, and what little I'd eaten of lunch felt like a boulder in my stomach.

How could my best friend say those things about me?

8

The Companion
Confrontation

"SO, AFTER SEEING THAT CLIP, HOW DO YOU
feel?" Joey asked me.

"Uh . . ." I slowly shook my head, my mouth still wide
open. "Stunned."

Noah was supposed to be my best friend. Is that
what he really thought about me? He had to have been
showing off for the show. But why would he say those
things when he knew I felt the exact opposite? Maybe
he didn't really believe me?

"Care to elaborate on that?" Joey asked, interrupting
my runaway train of thought.

"I don't know," I said with a big sigh. "I thought he was my best friend."

Joey winced. "That doesn't sound like something a friend would say, let alone a *best* friend."

There was another awkward silence as I stared blankly at the camera, focused on the little red recording light just to the left of the lens. Suddenly, I felt embarrassed to be in the makeshift room. I wasn't about to cry or anything, but I could feel the camera capturing every inch of devastation on my face. I had to get out of there.

"Excuse me," I said, standing up and moving toward the curtain.

Joey switched off the camera. "We'll pick this up another time, then?"

I gave a quick nod as I drew back the fabric. "Okay." Grabbing my lunch tray and notebook, I hurried out of the room, back toward the cafeteria.

I must've been in a daze, because I hardly remembered dumping my tray, swinging by my locker, or heading to robotics class. Some classmates might have tried to talk with me in the hallways, but I couldn't remember who or if I answered them. I felt numb.

And worst of all, I knew I'd have to face Noah in

class. I didn't know what to say to him. Maybe I'd get lucky and he'd be off with one of the camera crews again.

No such luck.

As everyone filed into class, in came Noah followed by Sean and Mike, the other camera crew. As Noah put his stuff down on our worktable, I caught Sean recording us out of the corner of my eye. I tried to ignore them all.

When Noah pulled out his notebook and began writing, I focused on my robot, taking apart one of the arms so I could replace its rubber belts with slightly smaller ones. I hoped the new additions would make the arms more sensitive and able to handle simple tasks with greater ease.

I guess what I was doing was too boring for the show. Sean and Mike moved to another worktable on the other side of the classroom, where Mia Trevino was mixing a powdery substance with water in a bucket. It almost looked like she was making her own pancake batter. Except pancake batter wasn't supposed to be pink.

Meanwhile, Sam sat on a stool next to her. Sam removed her shoes and socks, rolled up her pants, and positioned two short, stubby cardboard tubes next to Mia's bucket. Since Mia's father worked in special effects for movies and TV shows, I could almost guess what they were doing: It looked as if Mia was getting ready to make casts of Sam's feet. My theory was confirmed when Mia poured the gloppy substance into the tubes and Sam slowly sunk her feet inside.

"Ooh," Sam said, wincing. "That's cold."

"Sorry," Mia said. "If I warmed the water, the alginate would harden faster."

Sean and Mike's attention (along with that of several other students) was focused on Sam and Mia. I didn't know what Sam's big project was, or how it related to Amy's gum recycling program, but it seemed that she needed casts of her feet.

"Hey," Noah said.

It took me a second to realize that he was talking to me. "Hey," I replied, going back to work on my robot.

"Thanks for making that lens filter," he said.

I gave a quick nod and began disassembling my robot's other arm. "I said I would."

Noah shifted on his stool. "Well, Joey said it works great."

"Good," I replied without looking up.

Noah made a few notes in his notebook, then put his pen down. "Look, I'm sorry I got so worked up about it. I should've known you would come through."

I let out a sigh, but still didn't look up. "Whatever."

Noah leaned forward, lowering his voice. "Hey, I'm trying to apologize here."

Why was he whispering? Was he afraid the camera crew would record him being nice to me?

"Fine," I said, glancing at him. "You apologized."

Noah sat straighter again and shook his head. "Man."

We didn't speak for the rest of the class. I focused on making adjustments to my robot; he kept scribbling notes.

I did occasionally check in on Sam and Mia's station. After Sam removed her feet from the tubes, she and Mia mixed what looked like plaster and filled the molds. By the end of class, they'd ripped open the cardboard tubes, revealing two white stone-like copies of my friend's feet and ankles.

As the rest of day went on, my hurt and disappointment slowly morphed into anger. I didn't realize it at first, but

I started keeping to myself even more as I stewed over what Noah had said. When I did have to interact with other students or teachers, my statements were short, and sometimes even gruff.

I didn't like feeling that way. My insides were wound up like a spring compressed to three thousand PSI. I wished I hadn't kept quiet with Noah in class. I wished I'd told him how I felt.

Just before last period, I decided to remedy the situation. I swung by Noah's locker, but I didn't see him. I ran up to the third floor, thinking I might catch him in biology. He wasn't there, either.

With Noah having a pocket full of hall passes and the run of the school thanks to his personal camera crew, there was no telling where he could be.

Then I remembered again what he'd said in the confessional. Maybe he was there, commenting on our last interaction. As I trudged down the stairs, I could just picture what he was saying:

"I tried to apologize to him, but Tom Swift's too stuck-up to listen. His name's on the school, so why would he care what any of us peons has to say?"

I grew angrier with each step.

When I got to the computer lab, I saw that Noah wasn't in the actual editing suite. Instead, he sat in front of one of the school computers. But one of the camera crews *was* with him, so I wasn't entirely off.

As I marched closer, I saw that Lori had her camera trained on the screen as Noah scrolled through lines and lines of code.

"Listen," I said.

Noah held up a finger. "Hang on a minute, man." He kept one finger on the keyboard, keeping the code slowly scrolling. "I didn't have many sketches for Amy to animate, so they're grabbing footage of my app code for one of their transitions."

I trembled with anger as he put me off. "What? Are you in charge of everyone now? You going after Davenport's job next?"

Noah stopped scrolling and looked up at me, a confused expression on his face. "What are you talking about?"

I gestured to the nearby camera crew. "I'm talking about the *Noah Newton Show* and how you're tearing people down to get to the top."

Noah pushed out of his chair and stood to face me. "Tearing people down?"

"You think I *want* to have the same name as the school? Do you know how much pressure that is?"

Noah nodded, eyes wide. "Yeah, you've literally told me that a thousand times."

"Well, apparently you don't believe me! You think it's all an act. You think I really want special treatment, right?"

Noah spread his arms wide. "Dude! Again . . . what are you talking about?"

I tapped my chest. "And *I'm* not a good inventor? Half of my projects were with you. How does that make any sense?"

"Who said you weren't a good inventor?"

"You did!" I snapped.

"What? No, I would never!"

"I *saw* you say it! I can't believe you'd deny it to my face." I threw up my hands. "You'd think the star of the *Noah Newton Show* would at least have the guts to own up to his words."

With that, I turned and stormed out. As I hurried down the hall, I realized that the camera crew had been recording our entire exchange.

At that moment, I didn't even care.

9

The Unwitting Escalation

"I THINK HE'S JUST JEALOUS," I SAID, LOOKING directly into the camera lens. "Do you know how many times he's told me what he would do if he was in my shoes?"

"Oh yeah?" Joey asked from his usual spot in the confessional.

"Yeah," I replied. "Noah's told me that he would totally take advantage of having the same name as the school."

After I got home from school the day before, I couldn't stop stewing about what my "supposed" best friend had said about me. Sure, I'd told him off—that had helped release some of my anger—but I needed more.

That's when I decided to fight fire with fire.

As soon as I got to school, I found Joey and offered to record another session in the confessional. After my previous reluctance, he was thrilled.

"I bet Noah would really like the school to be called the *Newton* Academy. No, he'd want it to be called the *Noah* Newton Academy, just so no one would think it was named after Sir Isaac Newton."

I had thought up that one the night before.

Joey nodded in approval. "That's great, Tom. Do you think any of the other students are jealous of you?"

The question took me by surprise. "Uh, I don't think so. At least no one has ever mentioned it."

"To your face." Joey chuckled.

"No," I agreed. "Have you heard anything?"

"Oh, I was just asking," Joey said, waving away the question. He glanced at his watch, then shut off the camera. "I think that's good for now. I have someone else coming in."

"Oh, okay," I said as I stood.

I suddenly didn't feel as fired up as I had when I went

looking for Joey. Actually, I felt a little childish venting about Noah. But as soon as I thought about what he'd said again, my lip curled. I hoped Joey showed Noah my video so he could see how it felt.

When Joey pulled back the curtain, I jumped. Amy was standing there dressed in full hazmat gear.

"You're scraping gum in here, too?" I asked.

"Nope." Amy closed her eyes, taking in a deep breath and letting out a long sigh. "I'm . . . doing an interview."

My eyes widened. "What? Really? You don't have to, you know."

Amy gave several quick nods. "I know . . . but I think I'm ready." A nervous chuckle escaped her tightened lips. "Push past your comfort zone, and all that."

I looked her up and down. "In full gear, too?"

"It helps," she replied. "Thanks for the idea."

"Ah, Amy," Joey interrupted. "Right on time."

She gave me a small wave before taking a seat in front of the camera. I couldn't believe she had actually agreed to be on camera by herself.

I left the editing suite to find Sam waiting in the computer lab. She grinned, jutting a thumb back the way I had come. "What do you think?" she asked. "Can you believe Amy's actually doing an interview?"

I shook my head, mouth hanging open. "And . . . the hazmat suit was my idea, somehow?"

Sam shrugged. "Well, it was."

"It was?"

Sam nodded. "Remember the fencing helmet?"

"Oh yeah."

A while back, when it looked like Amy's fencing team was going to be interviewed by a local news reporter, Amy had started having a full-blown panic attack at the thought of being the center of attention. I had suggested that she wear her fencing helmet to hide her face, and it had worked. I guess she thought her hazmat suit would do the trick too. If it had shielded her from being the center of attention in the cafeteria earlier, why wouldn't it work for just one camera?

I nodded toward the editing suite. "Have you gone in there yet?"

Sam rolled her eyes. "Yeah, once. Noah talked me into it."

"Did you talk about your new invention?"

"A little," Sam replied.

"Care to tell a friend what it is, since you were willing

to tell a perfect stranger? From what I saw yesterday, I'm guessing it has something to do with feet."

Sam shrugged. "It's not that big of a deal. I just thought I'd put off the ribbing as long as possible."

"Okay, one, now I'm superintrigued. And two, since when do I rib you about your inventions?"

Sam glared at me over the rims of her glasses. "Seriously, Swift?"

I held up a hand. "I mean, anything beyond good-natured goofing among friends."

"You know what was weird about the interview?" Sam asked, obviously changing the subject. "Joey didn't seem *that* interested in any of my inventions. He mainly asked a bunch of questions about other students. If I had any rivalries in school, stuff like that."

"Really?" I was too embarrassed to tell her that in my last interview I hadn't talked about my inventions once. I'd just vented about Noah.

"And that's not all," Sam continued. "Joey asked me a bunch of questions about you."

"Me? Like what?"

Sam shrugged. "I don't know. Things like how I felt

about your dad founding the school. Did you get special treatment? Stuff like that."

My lips pressed together and I felt another wave of anger wash over me. "I have a feeling Noah's the source of that topic." I told her about what my supposed best friend had said about me in the video clip Joey had shown me.

"Noah said that?" Sam asked. "I don't believe it. That doesn't sound like him at all."

"Oh, he denied it, but I saw the recording with my own eyes."

Sam shook her head. "Why would he do that?"

I didn't have an answer, and I didn't get a chance to respond anyway as the first-period bell rang. I reached into my pocket and pulled out a hall pass.

"You have another one of those?" Sam asked. "Amy asked me to stay with her for moral support."

I shook my head. "Joey still has tons of them, though. I'm sure he'll give you one."

I left the computer lab and made my way downstairs toward algebra. As I shuffled along, my mind kept going back to my conversation with Sam. Was news of Noah's and my argument so widespread that Joey was asking everyone about it? Boy, now I felt really stupid for going in there and fanning the flames of our argument. I had originally thought the Swift Academy's reality show would turn into the *Noah Newton Show*, but was it really going to be the *Tom Swift Show* and I was just the last one to find out about it? And had I just helped it along?

10

The Intention Assessment

I DON'T KNOW IF I WAS JUST BEING PARANOID,
but ever since Sam had mentioned Joey asking about
me, now it *really* felt like everyone at the school was
watching me. Before, it was nothing more than a casual
glance, but more recently, some of my classmates were
full-on staring before turning to whisper into a nearby
friend's ear. I felt as if everyone was waiting for me to
do something.

I'm sure I was just being oversensitive. Why would
anyone care what went on between Noah and me?
There seemed to be more and more drama to go around.

Everywhere I looked there were different sets of friends bickering or walking away from each other in a huff.

"I don't want to hear it," Anya Latke said as she brushed by me.

"Anya," Jenna Davis called out as she hurried to catch up to her friend. "I never said your program was stupid. Honest!"

I stopped to watch the squabbling students disappear into the flow of traffic. What was the academy turning into? It was as if the pressure of the reality show or the upcoming Inventors' Olympics was sending everyone over the edge.

I tried my best to ignore the rising drama level and go about my business like it was any other day. I did spot both camera crews trailing me at different points in the day. As usual, I did my best to be as boring as possible, keeping to myself and going to class. I hardly saw Sam or Amy. And who knew what Noah was up to. Part of me worried that I was going to become as introverted as Amy if I kept this up.

After the final bell rang, I swung by my locker, and then headed out to the academy's front lawn. I hadn't collected any loot on Noah's app, but I wanted to see if my classmates had found enough to finally satisfy the beast.

Things looked better already. Although the entire student body wasn't present, this was by far the biggest turnout yet. Each person held up their phone, waiting for the virtual monster to attack. I dug out my own phone and quickly found Sam and Amy farther down the lawn.

"Hey. How did your interview go?" I asked Amy.

She shrugged. "Okay, I guess. The suit helped but I was still sweating buckets during the whole thing."

"Yeah, it went great, all right," Sam added. "And then they fired her!"

"What?" I asked.

Amy shook her head. "They didn't fire me. I still get to help organize clips for Danny." She let out a long breath. "But Joey doesn't want me doing any more animations."

"But they looked so cool," I said. "That doesn't make any sense."

"I know, right?" Sam said, throwing her hands into the air.

"He said they were 'going in a different direction,'"

Amy continued. "From what I've seen so far, they're focusing more on the drama going on in the school."

"Yeah, what's up with that?" Sam asked. "Is it just me, or is everyone all worked up lately?"

Amy shook her head. "It's not just you. I've noticed it too. People are snapping at each other all over the place."

Sam crossed her arms. "And I'm sure the camera crews are getting it all on film."

Amy nodded. "They are."

I was embarrassed to tell my friends that my argument with Noah would be a big part of that school drama. The cameras had sure captured us bickering enough.

"What are they going to do with all the scanned images of everyone's notes and blueprints?" I asked, trying to change the subject.

Before Sam or Amy could answer, Noah charged over. "I saw your latest confession, Tom," he said with a snarl. "Nice. Real nice."

"What's he talking about?" Sam asked.

"Oh, he didn't tell you? My best friend here thinks I'm jealous of him," Noah snapped, jutting a thumb in my direction.

"What?" Amy asked.

"I just told the truth," I barked. I couldn't believe Noah had the nerve to be angry at me.

"Swift?" Sam said accusingly. "I don't believe you."

Noah nodded vigorously. "Oh, believe it. He thinks I want the school named after me instead."

I pointed at Noah. "Well, *he* thinks I'm a crappy inventor!"

Amy gasped. "Noah!"

He shook his head. "And I *still* don't know what you're talking about!"

Sam motioned for us to be quiet as she glanced around the schoolyard. Both camera operators were slowly pushing through the crowd, heading our way. "You better keep it down unless you want this to end up on the show," she whispered.

Amy looked toward the ground, fidgeting with her hands.

I had a lot more to say about Noah, but I didn't necessarily want it recorded for posterity. Sighing, I held up my phone, mimicking the other students around me. Noah glared at me one more time before doing the same.

Through my phone's screen, the beast slowly marched

toward the school. There was even an animated heli-copter hovering above its head this time. But if I'm hon-est, the new addition didn't really hold my interest. I was still fuming about Noah. *I can't believe he's still denying what he said about me*, I thought.

In my peripheral vision, I saw the camera operators slowly lose interest in our group; they turned to sweep their cameras over the rest of the crowd.

"I *saw* you say it," I whispered to Noah. "Why can't you just own up to it?"

"I would own up if I *had* said it," he hissed back.

"Maybe you just heard wrong," Sam murmured.

"You're taking his side, now?" I asked, my whisper getting louder.

Sam shook her head as she kept her eyes fixed on her screen. "I'm not taking anyone's side. I just can't believe Noah would say anything like that."

"Look, I said he was jealous," I admitted. "There. I owned up to what *I* said."

Noah shook his head. "And that's a low blow, man."

Amy whispered something, but it was so quiet, I couldn't make out what it was.

"What?" I asked her.

"I said, we can go see for ourselves," she repeated. "If it will get you two to stop fighting, I can find the clip you're talking about."

"Excellent idea." I glanced at Noah. "Last chance to come clean."

Noah nodded. "Oh, let's go settle this right now."

I looked around to locate the camera crews. They'd disappeared in the sea of students who were watching the virtual beast's approach. Without another word, the four of us eased out of the crowd and slinked back toward the school. I followed the others through the front door, with one last glance over my shoulder to make sure we weren't being followed. I'm sure the four of us sneaking away would've piqued the interest of the camera operators.

"I'll have Danny pull up the exact clip," Amy said as she led the way up the stairs to the second floor. "Then we'll see."

"We certainly will," I agreed, glaring up at Noah. He just shook his head and rolled his eyes.

Everyone followed Amy into the computer lab and into the adjoining editing suite. For the first time since I'd been to the new space, it was completely empty.

"He must be out watching the beast with the others," Sam surmised.

I looked over the complicated workstation. "Do you think you can find it, Amy?"

She sat down in front of the keyboard. "I think so. After all, I helped organize it."

Using the keyboard and the large trackball, Amy navigated to a screen full of file folders. She opened one labeled CONFESSIONALS, revealing more folders inside. Each of these had a student's name, just like the scanned blueprints. Amy scrolled down and selected one labeled NEWTON, NOAH. There were dozens of new files inside.

Sam gave a look of disbelief. "How many of these did you do? Have you even been to class lately?"

I sighed and shook my head. "Welcome to the *Noah Newton Show*."

"Just show me the clip you're talking about," Noah snapped.

Amy moved the cursor over the files. "How do you know which one it is?"

"It's Newton eleven," I said confidently. I may not have a photographic memory like Amy's, but I remembered the file Joey had asked for.

Amy clicked on the icon and Noah's smiling face appeared on the large viewscreen above the workstation.

"Get over yourself, Tom Swift," the Noah onscreen said. "Just because your name's on the school doesn't mean that you're a big deal."

Sam and Amy gasped in unison.

"Noah!" Sam said.

"Oh snap," Noah muttered. "I remember this now."

"You probably wouldn't be here if your dad hadn't built the school," Onscreen Noah continued. "You're not even that good of an inventor." The clip cut to black.

"There," I said, pointing at the screen. "Is that clear enough for you?"

Amy sprung out of her seat and rounded on Noah. "How could you?"

"What were you thinking?" Sam asked.

Noah held up his hands. "Okay, okay, I know this looks bad."

"It *is* bad!" Amy barked. I had never seen her so worked up. "Tom is your best friend!"

"Listen, I can explain," Noah said, backing away.

Sam narrowed her eyes. "I don't see how."

Noah pointed at the workstation. "Ames . . ."

"Don't you *Ames* me," Amy said, shaking her head.

"No, please. Is there a way to show the entire clip?"

Amy crossed her arms and just glared at him.

"Please?"

Amy let out a long breath and sat back down. She shook her head as she moved the cursor over to a screen showing a timeline of Noah's clip. Only part of the bar was highlighted. Amy moved the start point back and the end point forward. Once most of the clip was selected, she pressed the space bar so that it played on the main screen.

"Tell me about your friend Tom," came Joey's voice from the speakers. Since he sat behind the camera, his voice was softer than Noah's had been.

"Tom's great," Onscreen Noah replied. "He's a first-rate inventor, too. You should see some of the cool stuff he comes up with."

I suddenly felt very confused. Here was my best friend, in the same clip, saying how great I was. I didn't understand.

"What would you say are some of his faults?" Joey's offscreen voice asked.

On the screen, Noah glanced down. "I don't know. I

guess he gets hung up sometimes about people treating him differently because of his name."

I glanced over at Noah. He gave a small shrug and a nod in a *Well, you do* kind of way.

It was true. If anyone was sick of listening to my worries about being treated differently, it had to be Noah.

"Interesting," Joey's voice said. "What do you think Tom worries people would say to him if they thought he was getting special treatment?"

Onscreen Noah rubbed the back of his neck nervously. "I don't know . . . probably something like"—he straightened and looked right into the camera—"'Get over yourself, Tom Swift. Just because your name's on the school doesn't mean that you're a big deal. You probably wouldn't be here if your dad hadn't built the school. You're not even that good of an inventor.'" Noah shrugged. "Something like that, I guess."

"That's great," Joey's voice replied. "I think that's all we need for now."

The screen went black as the clip ended.

The four of us blinked at one another, stunned.

Sam pointed to the screen. "So, Joey just showed you *that* part?"

I nodded.

Amy covered her mouth. "How awful."

My face grew warm as I felt both embarrassed and angry at once—angry for being so easily manipulated, and ashamed for being so upset with Noah that I'd said horrible things about him. At least Noah hadn't meant what he'd said. I had.

I could barely look at my best friend. "I'm so sorry, man."

Noah held up a hand. "No, I'm sorry. And I would be furious too if I saw that clip."

"Yeah, but the stuff I said—"

Noah held out a fist. "Don't worry about it."

I smiled and bumped his fist with mine.

"Okay, we get it. You're both friends again," Sam said, shaking her head.

Amy covered her mouth and giggled.

"The bigger issue here is that you were being manipulated into hating each other." Sam nodded at the workstation. "Since there are so many people at each other's throats, do you think Joey has been doing this to everyone?"

Amy's fingers raced over the keyboard. "I can find out."

Just then, we heard voices coming from the computer lab.

"Both camera crews lost them," Joey said, his voice getting louder. "But they'll pick them up tomorrow."

The four of us exchanged looks. We were trapped with no way out.

11

The Obliteration Objective

"IN HERE," I WHISPERED, PULLING BACK THE curtain to the confessional.

We crammed into the small area. It was tight with four of us and all of our backpacks, but I was just able to pull the curtain closed again.

"Wait a minute." Amy shoved past me and hurried back to the workstation.

My heart raced as I watched her lean over the keyboard. Joey could walk in at any moment. Amy quickly closed out Noah's video clip, and then backed out of all the open folders. Soon the screens matched the way we had found everything. At least, I assumed they matched. Amy was the one with the photographic memory, after all. She pushed in the chair and then scurried back to us in the confessional.

No sooner had I closed the curtain again than I heard Joey enter the room. "I'll get Tom in the confessional again first thing in the morning. We'll show him Noah's new clip. You have it cut down already, right?"

"All done," I heard Danny respond.

I shot Noah a questioning look. He shrugged and winced in reply.

"Great," Joey said. "Now, show me where you are with the new narrative."

There was the sound of tapping keys before the speakers boomed with dialogue:

"Everyone's very competitive at Swift Academy," came a girl's voice. I think it was Jessica Mercer. "We're always trying to top each other."

The background sound changed to that of a busy hallway. "You totally stole my idea," said Toby Nguyen's voice.

"That's not true," replied Ronny Jenkins's voice. "My invention is completely different. Besides, you said you were done with drones anyway."

I probably wouldn't have recognized Toby's and Ronny's voices, but I had seen that exact exchange a few days earlier.

The background noise shifted again, and another student's voice filled the room: "If Barry thinks I'm doing all the work on this project, he better forget it."

"She's just mad that I thought of the idea first," came a boy's voice from a different scene.

Hiding next to me, Sam shook her head in disgust. I felt the same way. Danny had edited the footage to make it seem as if the whole academy was constantly squabbling. Sure, there were disagreements sometimes, but nothing like this. Thinking back to Noah's footage, I wondered how many of those disagreements were incited by Joey himself.

"There's one person to watch out for, though," said another girl's voice.

"Tom Swift," said a boy's voice.

"Tom Swift," repeated a girl.

"Tom Swift," echoed another boy.

I looked at my friends in disbelief. They met my gaze, wide-eyed.

I couldn't help myself. Slowly, I peeked my head out

from behind the curtain just enough to glimpse the back of Joey's and Danny's heads as they watched the main screen, where Jamal Watts was sitting in the confessional.

"Tom's dad created the school," he said. "He also owns Swift Enterprises next door."

The scene cut to a shot of Jim Mills. "That's where I built my roll cage," Jim said. "But I could only finish it during the school's lock-in."

Next was Evan Wittman. "I bet Tom has access to all the cool equipment over there anytime he wants."

Then the video cut to an all-too-familiar clip. "Get over yourself, Tom Swift," Noah said. "Just because your name's on the school doesn't mean that you're a big deal."

As the screen went blank, I was so shocked that I kept my head poked out from behind the curtain, my mouth wide open. Luckily, Sam pulled me back into the confessional before either of the men could turn and see me.

"Excellent," Joey said. "And I already told Sean and Lori to get some more footage along the same narrative."

I didn't hear the rest of their conversation. I was too

horrified by what I'd already seen and heard. Not only were they making our school seem as if it were full of bickering brats, but they were making me out to be the biggest brat of all. A big part of me wanted to rip back the curtain and confront the film guys right then and there, but before I got the chance, I heard their voices trailing off. They must've been leaving the editing suite.

After a long moment of complete silence, Sam whipped the curtain back. "Unbelievable!"

"That's horrible," Amy said, shaking her head.

Noah put a hand on my shoulder. "I'm so sorry, man."

"It's all right," I told him. "I saw how you were manipulated into saying that stuff."

After watching Noah's entire clip, I knew he didn't mean any of the rotten things he had said. What troubled me more was what everyone else had said on film. Did all of the other academy students really think of me that way?

"I can't believe what everyone else said, though," I muttered.

Sam stared at the workstation, her hands resting on her hips. "You said it yourself, Swift. Noah was manipulated into saying those things. I bet everyone else was too." She let out a long breath. "Now . . . can you delete everything, Amy?"

"What?" Amy asked.

"What?!" Noah and I echoed.

"Just get rid of all that garbage," Sam said, swiping her hand through the air. "Delete the whole thing."

I suddenly noticed Sam's body language. If there were a baseball bat handy, I bet it would have taken all three of us to keep her from smashing the entire setup.

"Whoa, Sam," Noah said. "I get that you're angry. I know I am. But that's someone else's stuff."

Sam rounded on him. "That's us. All of us! If anyone has the right to delete it, we do."

I shook my head. "Noah's right. We have to do . . . I don't know, something, just not that."

"We could tell Mr. Davenport," Amy suggested.

"Good idea," I said. "He thinks this show is going to promote the school. If he knew what it was really about, he would stop it right away."

Sam pursed her lips. "Fine."

"If we hurry, I bet we can still catch him," Noah said, heading toward the door.

But as I followed the others, a thought popped into my mind. I turned and surveyed the suite. "Hey, Amy . . . where's that hard drive with everyone's plans?" I suddenly didn't want those TV people to have access to my blueprints or anyone else's. They didn't deserve to even look at them.

Amy came back into the room and looked around both workstations. "I don't see it." She crouched to look under the desks. "Maybe they moved it."

"All right," I said, heading for the door again. "First things first."

The four of us jogged downstairs to the main office. Ms. Lane wasn't at the reception desk so we breezed by, straight to the principal's office. Luckily, we caught Mr. Davenport just as he was about to head out for the day.

"Ah, you four," he said. "It's never good when you come to see me together." He raised an eyebrow. "What burned down?"

"This school's reputation, for one thing," Sam said as she marched inside.

"What?" Mr. Davenport asked as we followed her inside.

"We just saw a clip of the 'reality' show," Noah said, making air quotes as he said "reality." "And it's anything but real."

The four of us took turns telling Mr. Davenport what we had seen. Actually, just three of us. Amy only added the occasional "It's horrible."

The principal raised his hands. "Whoa, slow down. Joey warned me this might happen."

"He did?" I asked.

Mr. Davenport nodded. "He said that the show was going to be more than just inventions. He said it had to be . . . what did he call it . . . character driven."

"But it makes it look like everyone's fighting," Sam insisted.

Mr. Davenport shrugged. "Not everyone gets along all the time."

"Yeah, but we think Joey's starting fights to begin with," Noah added.

"Really?" Mr. Davenport said with a raised eyebrow. "Did he make any of you read from a script? I know I didn't during my interviews." He glanced at his watch and grabbed his briefcase.

"But it's the way they're editing everything together,"

Amy said, finally jumping in to support our argument.

Mr. Davenport was already moving toward the door again. "Look, I'm sure not everyone will be thrilled with how they appear on camera." Mr. Davenport held out a hand, ushering us out. "It's called a reality show for a reason. Sometimes reality isn't as neat and tidy as a scripted program."

Once we were back in the hallway, he turned and locked his office door. "I really have to be going, but I'll ask Joey about it tomorrow, don't you worry."

Then Mr. Davenport walked out of the school and left us standing in the main entryway, dumbfounded.

"He didn't believe us," Amy said.

Sam threw up her hands. "See? We should've deleted everything."

"It looks like Davenport fell for the hype like I did," Noah said.

"We all did," Amy admitted.

"What about your dad?" Sam asked me. "He'll believe you, right?"

I nodded. "He should."

"Well, that's it, then," Noah said. "He'll put a stop to this."

"Okay," I agreed. "I'll tell him tonight and then text you what he says."

The four of us split up. As usual, I strolled down the street to Swift Enterprises. I often hung out there and finished my homework before my dad took me home. It was a very convenient arrangement for both of us.

As I walked toward the looming office building, my mind went back to all the things the other students had said about me on the video. If I went running to my dad to fix this problem, I would be exactly the kind of person those students said I was. Whether my classmates were manipulated or not, I didn't want to come off that way. Besides, my father has told me in the past that he didn't have any say in how Mr. Davenport ran the school. Perhaps telling Dad wasn't the answer after all.

By the time I entered the office building, I already had a plan B in mind. I marched toward the reception desk. Mr. Cruz sat in his usual spot, typing on his keyboard. The thin man smiled when he saw me.

"Afternoon, Tom. Your father told me to tell you that he's in a meeting and he'll find you when he's done." Mr. Cruz pulled out a visitor's badge and slid it across the counter.

"Thanks," I said. "Actually, can you tell me where Ms. Jensen's office is? I've never been to the PR department."

"Oh," Mr. Cruz said, his eyebrows raised. "I guess you haven't heard. Ms. Jensen is no longer with the company."

So much for plan B.

12

The Simultaneous Simulation

THE NEXT MORNING, I HAD MY DAD TAKE ME TO school early. I hadn't told him about the reality show, much to the frustration of my friends. We had all video-chatted the night before, and I finally convinced them that there had to be a better way to stop the show. After some brainstorming, I think we had it.

As soon as I arrived, I stowed my gear and then ran up to robotics. I made sure my robot was fully charged and brought it with me down to the editing suite. As I'd hoped, Danny and Joey were already there.

"Tom," Joey said, his eyes alight. "Just the man I want to see."

"Hi," I said as I hauled my robot toward the confessional. "I was hoping to talk about my new invention today."

"Oh, uh . . ." He stroked his beard. "Actually, that's something for the other camera crews. In here, we just record your thoughts and feelings about everything."

"Oh," I said, trying to look disappointed. "Actually, the real reason I brought it along is because I was hoping to hide it here."

"Hide it? From whom?"

"Noah," I replied. "He threatened to tear it up the next time he saw it."

A smile pulled at Joey's lips. He held up a finger. "Hold that thought," he said before ushering me to the chair in front of the camera. Once he was seated beside the camera, he turned it on. "Okay, tell me again. Why do you want to hide your robot?"

I repeated what I'd said before. "Noah said that the only reason I got the idea for it was because of his app."

Joey nodded thoughtfully. He couldn't hide his delight. "And how do you feel about that?"

"I couldn't believe it! Noah and I are supposed to be friends."

Joey turned toward the curtain. "Danny, play back Newton fourteen, will ya?"

"You got it," Danny replied, and the screen beside the camera snapped on. It showed Noah in the confessional.

"Me? Jealous of Tom Swift?" Noah on the screen asked. "Did he invent a cool app that everyone in the school is using? I don't think so."

Noah had already warned me about what he'd said in his last confessional. He felt horrible about it. It was recorded just after Joey had shown him what I had said about him, so not only did I totally understand his anger, but I was also prepared. The recording wouldn't catch me off guard like last time. Noah and I had even worked it into our plan.

The image of Noah onscreen jumped as if part of the scene had been cut out. "He wouldn't even have that robot if it weren't for me," Noah continued. "He totally got the idea for it from my app." The video switched off abruptly.

I nodded. "Yup. That's what he told me yesterday."

"And what would you say to him if you could?" Joey asked.

I tried to look angry. "I'd tell him *so what*? I don't see *him* building a cool VR robot. He's just a programmer afraid to get his hands dirty. If he tried to build something like I have, it would probably blow up."

None of that was true, of course. Noah was a first-rate engineer *and* a top programmer, as far as I was concerned. But I needed to give Joey what we thought he wanted.

"That's great," Joey said. He made some notes in his notebook. "Now, do you think any of the other students are jealous of—"

"Actually, I have to go," I interrupted. I pretended to check the time on my phone as I stood. "Can we pick this up later today?"

"What? Oh, okay," Joey said, closing his notebook. "But definitely make some more time for this. It's very important to the show."

"I will," I agreed as I pulled back the curtain. "And thanks for keeping my robot safe."

"Oh, I will," Joey said.

Yeah, right, I thought. He'd probably love to have a clip of Noah messing with it for his not-so-real reality show.

I left the computer lab and went down to algebra. I couldn't wait to tell my friends how smoothly everything had gone. Unfortunately, when I walked into class, I realized that I'd have to keep my mouth shut. One of the camera crews was already there, watching—recording. Still, I gave Sam and Amy a subtle thumbs-up as I sat down.

I couldn't communicate with Noah. We were still supposed to be feuding after all. I wouldn't be surprised if that's why the crew was waiting for us in our first-period class. Joey probably texted them to find Noah and me and wait for some kind of blowup.

They didn't get one, though. Noah and I simply ignored each other completely.

During our chat the night before, Noah thought it would be fun to come up with some scripted arguments for the cameras, but Sam quickly talked him out of it. It would be much easier to pretend to give each other the silent treatment than to go for an Academy Award–winning performance with zero rehearsal time.

The camera crew stayed in class for the entire period, so we had no choice but to keep up the act. After class, they trailed after Noah, so at least I could talk to Sam and Amy.

"Everything still a go?" Sam asked as we walked down the crowded hallway.

"You bet," I replied. "We just have to keep cool a couple more hours."

Amy squeezed the straps of her backpack. "This is so stressful."

"Just act natural," Sam told her.

Amy rolled her eyes. "When someone tells you to act natural, that's the *last* thing you can do."

We split up and headed to our second-period classes. We just had to hold it together until the end of third period. Since Amy had been working in the editing suite, she knew that was when Danny and Joey would leave for lunch. And since they always left the campus to eat, they also locked the editing suite while they were away. Luckily, we had a man inside—well, a robot inside.

Just before the end of third period, I used one of Noah's hall passes to get out of class. I hustled down to the cafeteria and found Sam and Amy already waiting.

"Where's Noah?" Sam asked.

"I don't know," I replied, pulling the VR gear out of my backpack. I placed a controller in each hand and pulled my glasses down over my eyes. It took a few seconds, but I easily connected to my robot through the school's Wi-Fi network.

Noah finally arrived. "Man, I had a hard time ditching the camera crew. What did you tell—" He paused and sniffed the air. "Cool! Tater tots!"

"Focus, Noah," Sam scolded.

"All right, all right," Noah said as he pulled his tablet from his backpack. He gave the screen a few taps. "I'm tied in."

I glanced at my friends. "Time to go live."

I pressed a button on my right controller and my view shifted. Instead of just looking at a blank cafeteria wall, I now saw the interior of the editing suite. If I were wearing true VR goggles, it would look as if I was really there, but since I viewed the scene through my glasses, I saw a transparent version of the room. Fortunately, the image would be solid on Noah's tablet.

"How's it look?" I asked him.

"Crystal clear," he replied. "And recording."

I moved the joystick on my left controller to make the robot rotate left and right. The camera scanned the area. Once I was certain the room was empty, I moved the robot toward the main workstation.

"Okay, let's start with the same clip we saw yesterday," I said.

"Tap any key to wake the computer out of sleep mode," Amy instructed.

I raised my right hand and the robot's right arm came into view. I reached out and had its claw tap the space key. The bank of monitors blinked on. Then I reached over to operate the trackball. Unfortunately, I didn't take into account the smoothness of my robot's claws. Whenever I tried to roll the ball, the claw simply slid off the ball's polished surface.

"Uh-oh," I said.

"You'll have to use the keyboard," Amy said. "Press Command and Tab at the same time. Then press the down arrow three times before—"

"Hang on." I had barely gotten both claws over the keyboard. "What were the first two again?"

"Better let her drive, Swift," Sam suggested.

I nodded. "I think you're right."

"What?" Amy asked as I handed her the controllers. "Oh, okay."

I gave her a crash course before placing the glasses on her head.

"This is interesting," she said as she moved her hands in front of her face. On Noah's tablet, the robot's arms mirrored her motions. She giggled. "But *so* cool."

"Now *you* focus, Amy," Sam said, sounding slightly annoyed.

"Right," Amy said as she moved the robot closer to the keyboard.

After a couple of misses, Amy picked up the controls like a pro. Sam and I crowded around Noah's tablet and watched the claws nimbly tapping all the right keys. Above them, one of the screens showed the familiar file folders opening. It didn't take long before the large television monitor played the clip from the day before. Amy backed the robot away to better frame the screen while the video's sound played from Noah's tablet. That was thanks to a microphone I had added just for the occasion.

Sam shook her head as she watched the clip again. She seemed equally disgusted the second time around.

"Wait until Davenport sees this," Noah said with a grin.

"It may not be enough, though," I said. "You think we can find another clip that's equally as bad?"

"From the way this guy was stirring things up," Noah said, "I guarantee it."

Once the clip had finished, Amy moved the robot back to the keyboard. She tapped some more keys (even faster now) and another clip played on the big screen.

As she backed the robot up to get a better shot, all of us jumped with a start. It wasn't what was on the screen that had scared us. It was the giant face looming in front of it: Joey's face.

"What have we here?" Joey's voice asked through the tablet's tiny speaker.

13

The Reality Revelation

"IS THAT YOU, TOM?" JOEY ASKED, HIS FACE moving even closer to the camera. "I don't think you'll have to worry about Noah tearing up your robot . . . because I'm going to do it first." He gave a devious grin. "What do you think about that?"

I sprinted for the cafeteria door, then bolted into the hallway and raced toward the computer lab. In that moment, I didn't care if we had recorded enough footage to show Mr. Davenport. I just didn't want anything to happen to my invention. I didn't know Joey well, but from what I had seen so far, he might just be the kind of person to make good on his promise to destroy my robot.

I ran through the computer lab and burst into the editing suite. To my surprise, Joey was sitting casually in the chair in front of the workstation.

"I thought that would get you here in a hurry," he said with a huge grin.

I glanced at my robot; it was still thankfully in one piece.

Joey hit a key on the keyboard and the large television screen went dark. "So, you thought you'd get a sneak peek at the show, huh?" He clapped his hands together. "Spoiler alert! It's great, isn't it?"

"It's awful," I said. "You make it look like everyone's fighting all the time."

Joey gave a dismissive wave. "Come on, that's no big deal. You have to have some drama," he explained. "A show *just* about a bunch of young inventors?" He pretended to nod off. "Snoozefest."

"What about all that stuff about me?" I asked. "It looks like the whole school is against me."

Joey shrugged. "Hey, every great story needs a villain, right?"

I gasped. "A villain?"

"Okay, maybe 'villain' is a strong word." He snapped his fingers. "How about . . . 'antagonist'?"

"But why—"

"Look," Joey said, cutting me off. "In this story, Noah is the protagonist and you're the antagonist. It's simple. It's elegant. It's . . . Storytelling 101."

I couldn't believe what I was hearing. This guy was making me into the bad guy at my own school.

"But . . . it's not real," I muttered.

Joey chuckled. "I'm going to let you in on a little secret." He glanced around as if he was worried someone would hear. "Reality television . . . isn't real. None of it is." He pointed to the workstation. "I can have Danny cut that footage together in a hundred different ways to tell a hundred different stories. Reality television is all in the editing, my friend."

My lips pressed together. "And your manipulations."

Joey shrugged. "Well . . . a little push here, a little nudge there, maybe. But that's why I'm the best." He gave me a sly wink. "But come on. I didn't put words into anyone's mouth."

He was right about that. It was troubling how

easily my fellow students and I were pitted against one another. But that still didn't make it right.

"What do you expect Mr. Davenport will think about your show when he sees this?" I asked.

"Oh, please," Joey said with a smirk. "We have so much footage of him, he thinks it's going to be the *Ronald Davenport Show.* You know? 'Captain at the helm' sort of thing."

"Let's go get him," I suggested, crossing my arms. "Show him what you've been working on."

Joey motioned toward the door. "Be my guest. Danny and I put together a special cut just for him." He rolled his eyes. "It won't make it into the final show, but . . ."

"He'll have to see the final show sometime," I said. "What about then?"

Joey laughed. "Are you kidding me? By the time this thing airs, I'll be on a boat in Scotland searching for the Loch Ness Monster." He shrugged. "Maybe we'll even find it. I haven't decided yet."

This guy might actually win. Sure, we could show our recorded clip to Mr. Davenport, but one, Joey would probably find some way to explain it away, and two, we would probably get into trouble for using my robot to spy in the first place.

I had almost resigned myself to being the villain in this new reality show, when a knock at the door interrupted my train of thought and Mr. Davenport entered the room.

Perfect timing.

Joey leaped up from his seat. "Ron! You're just in time. I was telling young Tom here about some great footage we have of you."

"Actually, Mr. Davenport—" I began.

"It's rude to interrupt, Mr. Swift," the principal said with a sharp look. He softened when he turned back to Joey. "I'm sure it's nothing, but I heard some concerns from a few of the students on how they've been portrayed in your program."

Joey shot me a look. "Is that so?"

Mr. Davenport waved him away. "We'll get to that later. Let's see that footage you were talking about."

Joey smiled and plopped down at the workstation. "Coming right up, Ron," he said as his fingers flew across the keyboard.

Mr. Davenport turned to me and smiled. "I'm sure

it's a real *captain at the helm* sort of thing. Perfect for the *Ronald Davenport Show.*"

Joey froze mid-keystroke. "I don't know what you heard . . . ," he began as he slowly turned toward the principal.

"I heard and *saw* plenty," Mr. Davenport said.

I suddenly had the feeling I was being watched, and not by a camera crew. Glancing at the door, I saw my three friends peeking in at us. When Joey followed my gaze, Noah held up the tablet and wiggled it a little. The screen showed us in the editing suite from the robot's point of view. When Joey turned from the tablet to the robot, Amy gave a friendly wave and the robot mirrored her movements.

Mr. Davenport crossed his arms. "Now, let's see some *real* footage from the show."

"Come on, Ron," Joey pleaded. "It'll be out of context."

Our principal shook his head. "I don't care. Let's see it."

Amy leaned in and pointed to the workstation. "There's one already cued up." Behind us, the robot pointed along with her.

Joey shot her a *Thanks a lot* look as he pressed the space bar.

The main video monitor played the sequence we had

already seen—the one where everyone was hounding me. Mr. Davenport shook his head as he watched the clip run.

"You see, every good story needs a vil—an antagonist to . . . ," Joey began.

"Yes, I heard," Davenport said. "Play another one."

Joey opened another folder and selected a file. A new clip appeared on the screen.

"Did you hear what Terry said about you?" Ashley Robbins asked Deena Bittick as they walked down the hallway.

The scene cut to Terry Stephenson in the confessional. "Deena can be super stuck-up sometimes."

"Were you ever going to actually show our inventions?" Sam asked Joey. "I know your camera crews recorded them."

Mr. Davenport raised a hand. "I'll handle this, Miss Watson." He removed his glasses and rubbed the bridge of his nose. "I've seen enough."

Joey stopped the video. "You see, you need a little drama to move the story along," he explained.

Our principal checked his watch. "You and your people have exactly fifteen minutes to get off my campus before I have security escort you out."

"Yes!" Amy shouted, before catching herself and covering her mouth. The nearby robot mimicked her.

"You can't do that," Joey said as he leapt to his feet. "We had a deal!"

"For a show that makes my students look like spoiled brats?" Davenport asked. "I don't think so."

Joey shook his head as he began gathering his jacket and notebooks. "You're going to regret this. My lawyers are going to have a field day."

Mr. Davenport pointed to Noah's tablet. "Even after they see your detailed description of reality television?"

Joey shook his head and moved toward the door.

Then it hit me.

"Wait," I said. "Where's the hard drive with everyone's invention plans?"

Joey glanced back into the room before shrugging. "I don't know, kid," he replied. "That was Holly Jensen's big idea. I think she swung by and picked it up." Then he chuckled. "And if I know Holly, you have bigger problems than my little show."

I looked at my friends' stunned faces. I clearly wasn't the only one who didn't like the sound of that.

"Well, that's just great," Noah said.

14

The Augmented
Exhibition

"AS YOU CAN IMAGINE, IT WAS A DIRTY JOB AT
times," Sam said, pointing over to Amy, who was once
again dressed in her full-body hazmat suit. Amy held
a bucket in one hand and a paint scraper in the other.
The audience laughed as Amy gave the scraper a brief
wave. "But thanks to Amy Hsu, Swift Academy is now
gum free."

The spectators filling the bleachers applauded
Amy's presentation. She and Sam stood on a small
stage in front of the track. One of Amy's chewing gum
receptacles shared the stage and a large banner fluttered

in the wind above them. It read SWIFT ACADEMY INVENTORS' OLYMPICS.

Amy grabbed the receptacle and left the stage as Sam continued her presentation. "As for my invention, I took Amy's processed gum and recycled it into these custom sandals." She pointed down to her bright green footwear. "As you saw in the video, Mia Trevino helped me make casts of my feet so I could mold the melted material perfectly." She raised one foot off the ground. "And they're the most comfortable shoes I've ever worn."

The audience applauded again as Sam made her way off the stage. Noah, Amy, and I were waiting for her.

"So, let me get this straight," Noah said, rubbing his chin. "You're not supposed to step in gum . . . but now you're stepping in gum all the time?"

Sam jutted a thumb at Noah and raised an eyebrow at me. "See? This is what I was talking about."

I couldn't help laughing.

Noah raised his hands defensively. "No, no, I think they're cool. Still kinda nasty . . . but cool."

So far, the Inventors' Olympics had been a huge success. Jamal Watts and Maggie Ortiz had pitted two battlebots against each other, demonstrating how the academy hosted robot battles a few months back. Collin Webb did some stunt flying with his drone—the one everyone called the Collybird. And Jim Mills drove his custom hovercraft around the track. The audience seemed to love it. I know if I didn't already go to this school, I'd want to after seeing all the cool stuff we get to do.

"Come on, Amy," I said. "We're up next."

Ashley Robbins was just finishing up demonstrating her plastic water bottle shredder and recycler.

Amy pulled off her protective suit. "Ugh, I can't believe I agreed to do this."

"Come on! You're a natural," I said. "Besides, everyone's going to be watching the robot, remember?"

I had decided to showcase my robot after all. I was even going to have it make pancakes again. Well, it would do everything but the actual cooking. I wasn't planning on feeding everyone.

But the most brilliant part of my demonstration (if I do say so myself) was to have Amy pilot the robot. Like I said, she was a natural. She operated it flawlessly during our rehearsals. She could even crack an egg using both robot claws and not get any shell in the mixing bowl.

"This is turning out to be the *Amy Hsu Show*," Sam said.

"Yeah, this is her big night," Noah agreed. "Way to go, Ames."

"Oh boy," Amy said as she donned the VR gear.

"Please," I said. "Can we not add any more pressure before she helps with *my* presentation?"

They were right, though. Not only was Amy going to be on stage twice, but she had also received full credit for editing the short video that had launched events that evening.

Joey and his crew had left the school and all the editing equipment behind. The way things ended, I was surprised they let the school keep the editing suite as promised. Fortunately, my father's company ended up paying for the equipment, as well as siccing its legal team onto Joey's production company, just in case Joey wanted to make trouble.

But the most important thing Joey's guys had left behind was all of that raw footage. Amy had taken a week to cut together a cool video that really showcased the school. Best of all, the final video wasn't so *character driven* anymore. Heck, there wasn't even any dialogue. Music played over clips showing students happily building their inventions, collaborating, and testing them together. You know . . . just like how things really were at the academy!

"Next up, we have Tom Swift," Mr. Edge announced, "assisted by Amy Hsu."

The audience applauded as Amy and I took the stage. I carried the robot, while Sam and Noah brought up a small table with all the things we'd need to make pancakes.

"Hi, everyone," I said, trying to keep my nerves in check. "I originally created the glasses that Amy is wearing to help with Noah Newton's app, which you'll see in a minute. But then I realized that I could do more with them."

As I explained how everything worked, Amy had the robot begin making pancakes, just like we'd rehearsed. She measured out the mix, poured in milk, and then stirred it all together with a large whisk. The audience seemed most amazed when she cracked not one but two eggs without a hitch. There were more oohs and ahhs than at a fireworks show.

Amy finished the demonstration by pouring out a circle of pancake batter into a large frying pan. She had worked the robot flawlessly all around. She even made it wave at the audience as they applauded. I was proud of her. She was really pushing past her comfort zone tonight.

I waved a good-bye and as I was removing our equipment from the stage, I caught a glimpse of my father standing in the back. He applauded and then gave me two thumbs up.

Speaking of my dad, the case of the missing hard drive full of blueprints? That was easy. I found out from him that Holly Jensen was fired from his company for trying to steal company secrets. And when the police searched her home, they found the missing hard drive. Apparently, if she couldn't get secrets from my dad's high-security company, she was planning to sell invention ideas from the low-security academy next door. If they hadn't caught her, I might've seen my mathematical alarm clock in stores for Christmas!

Ms. Jensen's friendship with Joey had been real, which didn't surprise me given their similar lack of morals. But Joey had finally convinced the authorities that he had nothing to do with her corporate espionage. She had simply arranged the reality show as one big distraction.

Joey's lack of involvement also came as no big surprise, since he never showed interest in anyone's inventions, anyway. And from the way he explained how reality television worked, I think he could've made the exact same show at *any* school—just like the man said, cutting it together a hundred different ways if he wanted.

"Last up is Noah Newton," Mr. Edge announced.

I pulled out my phone as Noah took the stage. I noticed that I wasn't the only one. All the academy students had their phones up, knowing what was coming.

"Uh, hi," Noah said with a quick wave. "If you haven't already downloaded my app, this is your last chance." He pointed to the large television screen beside the stage. "Or you can watch what happens here."

While some stragglers quickly added the app to their phones, Noah explained what augmented reality was and how his app worked.

Sam gave me a nudge. "Did you download the update?"

"Definitely," I replied.

Noah had to make some last-minute tweaks before the big presentation. For one thing, he had to change the direction of the beast's attack, since everyone would now be gathered at the back of the school, instead of by the front. He also had to make it so he could trigger the beast's arrival. That way, his presentation wouldn't overlap with anyone else's.

"Okay, here we go," Noah said as he tapped the screen on his phone, then pointed it toward the eastern horizon.

Immediately, I felt the familiar footsteps vibrating in my palm. Sam, Amy, and I raised our phones and aimed them toward the east. I scanned the horizon until I spotted a tall figure lumbering through Shopton. From the murmurs coming from the audience, I could tell that most of them had spotted it too.

My phone vibrated harder and the chatter from the audience grew louder as the beast tromped into view. Even coming from a different direction, it made its usual beeline toward the school.

"Did you add any more animations?" I asked Amy.

"Wait for it," she replied, never taking her eyes off her screen.

Suddenly, my phone rattled in my hands as an old biplane buzzed overhead. The audience gasped in surprise as the plane motored toward the beast. I laughed as its machine gun opened fire on the giant creature.

"Good one," Sam said. "Just like in *King Kong*."

"Thank you," Amy replied.

As the plane zipped by, the beast swiped at it with its buzz-saw arm. The appendage connected and the plane blew up in a ball of fire. A few audience members clapped.

Then something else flew into the sky. A cartoon watermelon sliced through the air, falling short of the approaching behemoth.

"Too soon!" Noah shouted, shaking his head. "There's always someone."

A few academy students laughed, but everyone else held their fire.

The creature roared as it marched even closer. My phone nearly buzzed out of my hand with each step.

Then, just before it reached the school, Noah gave the order. "Now!" he shouted.

Suddenly, the sky was alive with lines of cartoon loot sailing toward the creature's mouth. There were giant cantaloupes, T-bone steaks, ham hocks, and comically huge strawberries. Every one of them streamed into the beast's mouth. Even though the spectators could merely watch the show, every academy student present launched collected loot from their phones. My phone vibrated again as the behemoth let out a loud belch.

The sky cleared, but the beast continued toward the school. I didn't understand. Noah and I had spent the day making sure all of the loot was collected. He told me about every hiding spot, and we made sure we collected whatever wasn't found by the other students. According to Noah's program, all of that should have been enough to truly feed the beast.

"I don't understand," I said. "That should've done it."

Amy glanced at me and rolled her eyes. "Noah's probably holding back. He told me he wanted to show some of the school's destruction to the audience."

Sam shook her head. "Show-off."

Just as before, the towering beast began cutting into the school with its spinning buzz saw. Sparks flew as chunks of the building fell away. I heard a few audience members gasp as large slabs of concrete seemed to hurtle toward them.

I glanced up at Noah just in time to see him tap his screen. I aimed my phone at him to see another line of loot stream away from his phone and toward the beast. The animated food items poured into the creature's mouth just before another belch made my phone vibrate.

Then something new happened. The beast halted its attack. It pulled a large white napkin from out of nowhere and dabbed at the corners of its grinning mouth. Then it tossed the napkin away and broke into a dance.

I laughed as a thumping beat blasted from my phone's speakers while the beast performed all the latest dance moves. It dabbed, flossed, and then went into a few routines that must not have gone viral enough for me to recognize.

The audience laughed and then erupted into cheers.

"Yeah!" I shouted as I joined in.

I caught Noah's eye and gave him a thumbs-up. He grinned back at me and danced along with the towering beast. I laughed so hard, I nearly dropped my phone. Sam and Amy joined me as we danced along with him.

I was thrilled for my best friend's success. He may not have become a reality star, but he was the star of this show!

READ&LEARN

with

simon kids

Keep your child reading, learning,
and having fun with Simon Kids!

A one-stop shop where you can
**find downloadable resources, watch interactive author
videos, browse books by reading level, and more!**

Visit us at
SimonandSchusterPublishing.com/ReadandLearn/

And follow us @SimonKids

SIMON & SCHUSTER
Children's Publishing

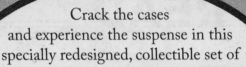

The City Spies are on the case!
From bestselling author
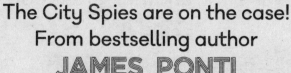
comes another must-read,
action-packed mystery series
that is sure to thrill.

Looking for another great book?
Find it
IN THE MIDDLE.

Fun, fantastic books for kids
in the in-be**TWEEN** age.

IntheMiddleBooks.com

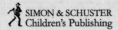